ASCELLA

by
Micah Chandler

The contents of this work, including, but not limited to, the accuracy of events, people, and places depicted; opinions expressed; permission to use previously published materials included; and any advice given or actions advocated are solely the responsibility of the author, who assumes all liability for said work and indemnifies the publisher against any claims stemming from publication of the work.

All Rights Reserved
Copyright © 2022 by Micah Chandler

No part of this book may be reproduced or transmitted, downloaded, distributed, reverse engineered, or stored in or introduced into any information storage and retrieval system, in any form or by any means, including photocopying and recording, whether electronic or mechanical, now known or hereinafter invented without permission in writing from the publisher.

Dorrance Publishing Co
585 Alpha Drive
Pittsburgh, PA 15238
Visit our website at *www.dorrancebookstore.com*

ISBN: 979-8-88527-289-6
eISBN: 979-8-88527-725-9

ASCELLA

TABLE OF CONTENTS

1. DUE TO PERSONAL REASONS, I'D LIKE TO BE HIT BY A TRUCK 7
2. BROKEN PROMISES AND PEANUT BUTTER CUPS 13
3. ANNA AND MANA ARE DRIVING ME BANANAS 22
4. I HATE PERFECT THINGS 31
5. DOG COLLARS AND KAWASAKIS 37
6. SO I GUESS I'M ANAKIN NOW 45
7. NATURE WOULD'VE LOVED ME BUT I RESISTED 56
8. I GIVE PANCAKES AND RECEIVE CREPES 73
9. IS MY BACK BLEEDING? I THINK I GOT STABBED 85
10. GRAB YOUR STICKS! I'M A PIÑATA! 92
11. PHOTOSHOP'S EVOLVED OR I HAVE AN IDENTITY CRISIS 114
12. DON'T EAT BURRITOS AROUND HALLOWEEN 124
13. I HATE THE ACT 132
14. CALM STREAM TO TSUNAMI 140
15. TAKE ME NOT HIM 150
16. I MESSED UP 162
17. GRANDMA'S CONDEMNING COOKIES 172
18. I HAVE BIG SLEEVES 179

CHAPTER 1

DUE TO PERSONAL REASONS, I'D LIKE TO BE HIT BY A TRUCK

"I'm really sorry," I said.

The little girl stared at me unanswering. Her eyes drifted from me to the broken window.

At least, I had a reason for shattering her window. It wasn't a good one, but it was better than nothing. Plus, I think I deserved a break after being the subject of a giant manhunt for a couple of days.

The little girl whimpered bringing me back to the reality of my situation. As much as I wanted to clean up the glass and apologize profusely, I had to get out of here before they showed up.

The glass shards crunched under my shoes as I walked back to the window and looked down. It was much too far to simply jump or step out; I had to fly. The little girl gasped as my wings unfurled.

"A-Are you an angel?"

I turned and smiled softly, hoping I wouldn't frighten her further.

"Not even close," I answered. "Can you do me a favor?" She nodded solemnly.

"Don't tell anyone I was here." She nodded again and I jumped out of the window.

I caught myself just as my fingers brushed the gravel and glided up into the air. Looking back, three pairs of eyes tracked me.

Crap! Her parents!

Sirens fired up in the distance.

Crap. Crap. Crap to the seventh power!

The flashing police lights came into view, and I veered off in the opposite direction.

"There!" A voice from below echoed.

To the left, a police cruiser rolled up.

I chuckled, "Big deal."

An engine revved to my right. Whipping my head around I saw seven, no, nine SWAT trucks.

Great.

I sped up, frantically searching for a way out of this mess. What sucks is when you go through one tragedy and then another one wants to jump on the boat too.

Hah! Try driving through this!

I soared over the border of the nature reserve park feeling like I'd gotten away, but the euphoric moment ended when a sharp pain hit my left wing and it started to drag. My body curled into a somersault and plummeted to the ground. Branches whipped across my face as I frantically grasped for a handhold. My fingers caught a branch, and I dug my nails into the bark.

CraaAAAAaack.

Crap to the eighth power.

~

I woke up on the ground with leaves and branches surrounding me. Throbbing pain flooded my entire body. Blood ran down the back of my shirt and I had a splitting headache.

"There he is!" a voice from behind me called out.

I rolled my eyes as the guns cocked.

Here we go again...

SWAT uniforms surrounded me. Shakily, I pushed myself

up and cursed. The damage was overwhelming enough without them honing in like bloodhounds.

"TR5," the one leading the squad said.

...and when I was so close to freedom.

A second guy stepped forward inserting a Tranquilizer dart into his gun.

"MOVE!" I screamed at myself. My wings twitched, but I lacked the strength to fly.

I looked back at the man who pointed the gun at me. I hated to accept it, but I was scared. What would happen if I was taken back?

"Please don't," I begged.

The gun drooped a little. He turned to the commander. "Sir, he-"

"Learn to follow orders!" the commander snapped, and in one swift motion, he yanked the gun from his subordinate and aimed the barrel at me. The shot echoed.

My shoulder jerked, and in a daze I looked down at the dart. The commander stepped forward and smirked. I spat at him causing him to do a double-take.

"I hate'chu," I managed to say, then the world went black.

~

I woke up on a cold surface and looked around the room.

What is this? A morgue.

Both my wings were stretched out and strapped to the table.

A lab.

I didn't even try to move. I could feel the restraints all over me. To my right, my reflection stared back at me from a mirror. If there was a pageant for the tired, mangled, and bloodied, I would have been a shoo-in for first place. Suddenly, the door opened, and a familiar scientist walked in. She leered as we made eye contact and sauntered over to me. She pinched my cheeks.

"Hey, handsome!" Dr. Anna said.

I wasn't sure if she was being sarcastic or just downright sadistic, but my whole body tensed.

"Just kidding," she clarified.

Nooo, my sarcasm kicked in as I regarded her sick humor.

"Don't worry, we'll fix you up once we're done but first..."

I hate you. I hate you. Just leave me alone!

".... the bullet in your wing. I don't want you half-dead for our next project." At first, I felt relieved, but then I read between the lines.

What if they "put me to sleep" and I never wake up!

I paused, death didn't sound so bad. At least it'd be over.

Dr. Anna walked away and picked up a syringe laying on the counter.

"What is that?"

"Just succinylcholine. Hang on, let me grab an IV."

She turned around and I yanked my wrists. The restraints loosed enough to make me try again.

Come on! Come on!

I glanced at Dr. Anna, who had her back to me still. Then the buckles clicked. I sat up, slipped my wrists out, and swiftly freed my feet.

"Will Collin Ascella!" Dr. Anna yelled.

I jumped off the exam table, but Dr. Anna guarded the door. The taser she gripped tightly caught my eye and I backed up.

Is there no way I can get her to move?

I picked up a cylinder of some random chemical and threw it at her feet. She deftly side-stepped it and the liquid sizzled and steamed on the ground. The doctor advanced. My back pressed against the wall and my injuries decided now was the perfect time to reopen. Blood dripped onto the ground.

The door opened and a new character stepped onto the scene. Mr. Lab Coat took a moment to analyze the situation before speaking.

"Why are you afraid, boy?"

He had a calm, but stern expression on his face.

"I'm not," I replied, thankful that my voice didn't betray me.

"Then why are you fighting?"

Why? Was Mr. Lab Coat an idiot? Oh I don't know, maybe 'cause ya kidnapped me!

"For my freedom."

I cringed; that was a really bad comeback.

"So you are afraid."

Um…maybe? I am stuck in a room with a bunch of psychotic madmen!

Immediately, I didn't like this man, he sounded like a frickin' psychologist.

The man opened the door and stepped aside, "There you go then, have your freedom."

"Mana!" Dr. Anna protested, but Mana held up his hand, cutting her off.

I decided to risk it and took a step forward. I waited for them to come grab me, but they didn't. Casually I walked out, and Mana shut the door behind me.

That was weird.

I looked down the hall and ran. It had been a good five minutes before I stopped myself. There hadn't been a single open window or door.

Could be a trap…but that would be too twisted, even for them.

I pressed my palm to my temple as the room began to spin.

Gas!

I cupped my mouth and nose, but it was too late. My knees buckled and I went unconscious.

CHAPTER 2

BROKEN PROMISES AND PEANUT BUTTER CUPS

"William!" my mother's voice echoed. "Will? Are you up yet?" It was the day I turned fifteen, nine months ago. Mom walked into my room as I sat gaping at myself in the mirror.

"Oh Will..." she said.

I turned back to my reflection.

"Does this mean I'm gonna be homeschooled?"

My mom's laugh filled the air.

"You have wings on your back and homeschool is what you're worried about?"

"Yes??"

We both walked downstairs, and I saw my dad at the stove cooking breakfast. He turned.

"Happy Birthday-"

He stopped short when he saw the black wings peeking out from my back. Suddenly, he smiled and raised his eyebrows.

"About time, I was getting worried!"

"What?" I needed a repeat, but then white speckled wings materialized behind my dad.

I jumped. That was unexpected, but it explained why I had wings.

"How do I make my wings disappear? I don't want to be homeschooled!"

"Son, I don't know if you can do that; you're part of your mother too."

The memory faded away, and I was once again pulled through the dark sea until I drifted to a different memory.

I relived homeschool and the nights with my dad teaching me to fly. But it was over, and the nightmare began. My parents and I were about to play Monopoly in the recreational room upstairs when the doorbell rang.

My dad went down while Mom and I waited upstairs. We could hear the door open, but it was loud. My mom jumped up the moment Dad yelled in alarm. Was someone breaking in? "Will, hide!"

I nodded and she disappeared downstairs. Mom's scream pierced the air, and I couldn't help but run down the stairs.

Whatever they'd done to my mother I couldn't forgive. Men in uniforms stood in my living room. I grit my teeth.

"Will, get out of here!"

I looked to my dad who had locked himself into a fight for control over a rifle. His white wings were out and the look in his eyes was one I'd never forget.

Sorry, Dad.

I went straight for the first guy who pulled out a pistol. He aimed at me and fired.

My mom pushed me out of the way just in time. She fell to the floor unconscious.

"Mom!" I screamed and ran to her side.

There was blood gushing from her chest.

I cradled her head in my lap unsure what to do. I didn't know how to save her.

"Let's go!"

I was pulled away by my dad who threw something at the window making it shatter. I was pulled through.

"Run!" my dad yelled. "Don't you dare stop!"

I looked at him with fear.

"Keep up!!"

I sprinted to keep up with my dad. We entered the forest behind our house. Suddenly, I was pulled behind a tree. I panted.

"Mom..." I whispered.

"Shhh, I know, I know son. But listen to me."

I looked up into his face and saw his eyes.

"No matter what, promise me you'll get away from here. These are bad people; they'll do horrible things to you."

I was going to answer, but Dad cut me off.

"Promise me," Dad whispered in my ear.

Tears streamed down my face as I nodded.

"Good," he ruffled my hair and smiled. "When I tell you, take off and fly as far away from here as possible and don't look back."

"What about you?"

"I'll meet you at the cedar."

The men were just on the other side of the tree. I wiped the tears from my cheek, looking at my dad who glanced at the men who were getting closer.

"Now."

He pushed me and I stumbled into a sprint away from the cover of the tree. An explosion erupted behind me. The fire lapped up the forest behind me and I stumbled over the roots in my path. I looked back to see the wall of light chasing me.

Dad...He promised he wouldn't let me down.

I turned and the moment I saw a clearing in the branches I took to the air.

He promised... I reassured myself.

The cedar tree on the hill came into view. Dad and I loved coming here, it was our safe haven.

He'd be here soon, I told myself.

I landed at the tree and looked back, wiping my tears.

"He won't let me down, Dad has always kept his promises," I whispered.

Suddenly, something hit my neck.

What?

I reached up to feel a dart.

How...

I pulled it out and felt my strength leaving.

How? They'd found me already!

It dawned on me a moment later.

Dad, you never intended to keep your promise, did you...

My eyes flew open, and I sat up abruptly. I looked around and saw that I was in a cell.

Lovely, back to square one.

White was probably the most creative color this room had. Directly across from me was a wall of tinted glass panels.

Probably escape proof, shatter proof, and bullet proof. My mind added the negativity that I just really needed right now.

I was about to get up, but pain flared in my shoulder from the sudden movement. I held it, bearing the pain with my other hand.

What did they do here?

A tracker wrapped around my ankle. I sighed and laid my head back against the wall as I closed my eyes.

"Crap to the ninth power," I grumbled.

"The ninth power?"

I jumped and looked at a man who was at the other side of the glass. He came inside and approached me.

"MR. LAB COAT?!" I snarled.

He ignored me and continued.

I scrambled to my knees in an attempt to get up. I leaned against the wall for support, and he moved closer.

I took a step and urged myself to move away, but I was too slow.

He was at arms length when I stumbled. I closed my eyes and tensed for the hard ground, but Mr. Lab Coat caught me.

The gloved hands lowered me to the ground.

"You're too injured to move right now; trust me."

Really? You want me to trust you?

Lab Coat crouched beside me.

"What more could you want from me? An autopsy?"

My voice was hoarse as I bit back bitter, hopeless tears. The doctor paused as he analyzed every detail of me.

"If we wanted to kill you, then we would've already done so."

I looked at him. He seemed genuinely concerned.

"Call me Mana, and I can assure you that as long as you're in my hands you're not going to die."

He stood up and I plopped against the wall. I watched as he walked out and closed the door. I should've been relieved, but I wasn't buying it. He'd already tricked me once.

I sat there for what seemed like hours, alone with my thoughts.

My eyes drifted shut and I thought about what Mana said. They were gonna make my death look like an accident.

"They're untrustworthy... They lied to me about the escape so why wouldn't they lie to me again. They don't want someone like me alive because I'm different. So they'll kill me for it. I need out. I want out. I'll -

My thoughts cut off when the door scraped open.

A boy, a bit older than I was, entered the room. He carried two trays of food with him. The aroma was overpowering, and my insides were gnawing on themselves for a bite. He hesitated.

"Hello," the boy quietly greeted.

I wanted to laugh. If this had been a different universe he would've been waltzing right into a monster's cave.

"Come near me and I'll kill you."

The boy froze, and his terror was all I needed to feel slightly happy.

"J.K."

The boy nervously chuckled. He came closer and sat down across from me. The tray stretched between us.

"I'm eating lunch with you today."

"No duh."

I didn't move as he awkwardly began eating without me. He looked at my blank expression and laughed to himself.

"The higher-ups call you the 'boy with wings'," the boy said bluntly.

"Do they?" I commented sarcastically. "Never would've guessed."

The blond smirked. "I'm glad someone around here has a sense of humor."

"Hah, don't even get me started," I laughed, picking up an apple and sinking my teeth into it.

CRRrrrrrrruuuuuunch.

"I'm Reece by the way."

"Like the peanut butter cups?"

"Uhm no."

I fought the obligation to tell him my name, but I talked myself into it.

"Call me Will."

Reece looked at me and straightened.

"I think I'm taller than you."

"That wouldn't surprise me."

"You just look taller sitting down."

"Maybe 'cause I have better posture than you," I replied smugly.

He rolled his eyes at the implied insult.

"How old are you?"

"Twenty-one."

"Well, I'll be," I drew out the words until they were practically dripping with sarcasm. "You're older, so maybe that's why you seem to be taller."

"And how old are you?

I ignored his question asking for my age and looked down. A sudden urge to stretch hit me, and my attention was drawn to my wings.

"I don't mean to be pushy, but could you possibly take these things off?" I pointed to the metal and leather straps keeping my wings furled.

"Sorry, Will."

I shifted to sit cross legged.

"So where exactly are we?"

"I'm not allowed to answer that."

I looked at him.

Reece remained silent.

"Can I ask who's in charge of-"

"Nope."

"Well, are you working with the government?"

"Will, I've been briefed NOT to supply information."

Wonderful, I just love that.

"So then basic?"

"Basic."
"Alrighty then, favorite color?"
Reece snorted.
"Green."
"Favorite animal?"
"Wolf."
Reece grinned as I kept shooting preschool questions at him, and he replied with short choppy answers.
"Favorite card game?"
"Spoons."
"Book series?"
"*Chronicles of Narnia.*"
"Sport?"
"Baseball."
"Favorite baseball team?"
"Classified."
I squinted my eyes at him.
"Just kidding, the Dodgers."
My eyebrows rose.
Well I guess everybody is different, I thought.
After a few more questions, I ended the questionnaire.
"You're weird, but you like *Doctor Who,* so you can't go wrong there. I guess you're okay."
He smiled and laughed at my comment.
"I have no words for you."
Finally, I cracked a smile.
"Now," he began acting as if he were a teacher. "It's my turn to ask you-"
Suddenly the intercom went off.
"Reece Ford," the monotone voice announced. "Your time has expired; please check in with the executive."
Reece grumbled what I thought was 'dang-it.'

He got up, grabbing the tray, and walked over to the door.

"Hey."

Reece turned around before he walked out.

"Bring some cards next time won't you? We'll get some games going in here."

Reece chuckled.

"Sure thing. See ya later, Will."

I nodded and waved slightly. Maybe this wasn't too bad.

Then he was gone, and I was alone again.

CHAPTER 3

ANNA AND MANA ARE DRIVING ME BANANAS

Once Reece left, time slowed down. To keep myself occupied, I picked at the tracker on my ankle and messed with the keypad by the door. I was sure the silhouettes on the other side found it just as amusing as I had when I'd come up with a tune from punching six, eight, and four repeatedly. I became bored with that rather quickly and paid attention to the moving shadows on the other side of the glass.

They're probably planning how to kill you, the voice inside my head suggested.

Shut up, I replied. I don't want to talk to you.

You're answering yourself.

Well, if you were locked in a cell for a few hours, I think you'd go crazy too.

Point taken.

Besides, at least I'm not answering myself out loud.

I sighed at my lunacy, but that was the extent of my concern.

Suddenly, a glass pane slid open, and that woman walked in.

"Come with me, Will."

Dr. Anna walked through, knelt down at my feet, and took hold of the tracker on my ankle. She did something and it fell to the floor. I didn't budge.

"Now."

As soon as we left, a couple of guards decided to accompany us to our destination. We passed through a few doors that led into different rooms, they all looked the same. I needed to get out of here, but the layout of this place was stupid.

Dr. Anna's voice snapped me out of my thoughts, "We're putting you through a physical examination," she said.

"What?" I mumbled, unamused, I'm not even close to being recovered.

However, Dr. Anna didn't seem to hear me and continued.

"We're going to check your health and run some tests, just to get some information on your physical stamina..."

Oooo, big words, I'm impressed.

She continued.

"...We'll run a few tests on your abilities..."

Eh, maybe this ain't gonna be too bad, just annoying.

"... and test your absolute threshold."

Wait, what??? Absolutely not.

She led me over to a scale, maybe to measure my weight. Doctor Anna-noying scribbled on her paper and walked back over to the counter.

"See that scale over there?"

I nodded.

"Stand on it."

We did this for about an hour which I found odd. She'd already poked and prodded me before. Why were we doing normal things now? My thoughts drifted back to my escape plan I'd begun earlier.

"There are highly trained officers outside if you plan to escape."

I stopped and looked at her.

So she can read my thoughts too? Well, crap to the tenth power.

"Okay, now for your wingspan."

I perked up. The bonds on my wings would be taken off.

Dr. Anna walked to the counter and grabbed a small remote. As she did, I hopped off the scale and stood awkwardly in the middle of the room.

She went to the door and opened it.

"Have Mana come in here; I'm about to evaluate his wings."

There was a grunt in reply, and she closed the door.

"Dr. Mana will analyze that bullet wound. But you should be fine."

Was she crazy? I was shot like two days ago!!

She must've recognized my confusion because she explained herself after studying me.

"You've got heightened healing. But I don't know the extent of it."

"Oh," I muttered. "Guess that just makes me fine and dandy then."

Suddenly the door opened, and Mana walked in, flashing me a smile.

"Will!" he said. "I'm so glad to see you. How are you feeling?"

"Absolutely spectacular!"

"Alright, that's good. I'm going to take this bandage off, okay?"

I nodded and stood still as he unwound the cloth and took a light out from his pocket.

"Unfurl your wings."

He clicked on the light as I did what he asked.

"Oh, this is good," he muttered, absentmindedly.

He turned the light off and placed it back in his pocket.

"You're all clear!" he said. "Those stitches are holding up well and the skin's closing."

"Thanks, Mana," Dr. Anna said.

"No problem, let me know if there's anything else."

He straightened and left the room. I heard a click and saw Anna had pointed the remote to the wall.

The technology she was controlling looked like a measuring device. It came down from the ceiling and stopped at the floor.

The heck was this??

"Stand on that 'x' please."

I took a small step forward and spread my wings across what I thought looked like a giant metal ruler. She took the measurements and walked away allowing me to stretch. My joints popped as I loosened my muscles.

I looked at the tips of my feathers and saw dry blood.

"Here."

I looked at the cloth the doctor held out to me. I took it and gave her a look before silently cleaning my wings.

She's much too observant.

Suddenly, I felt pain. My eyes were drawn to my left wing. Dr. Anna was holding one of my feathers in her hand.

"That HURT!!!" I growled.

"Sorry," she replied, insincerely. She got up and put my feather in her coat pocket.

I finished cleaning my wings just before she took the cloth from me.

"Why am I here?"

"You'll know in due time."

Why can't you be normal and answer the dadgum question!

Next were the minor tests, my blood pressure, reflexes,

etc. Basically, me sitting on the table, letting Dr. Anna's medical tingles take control.

My mind drifted to the memories of getting my physicals done for sports in middle school with my dad. Dad. I really missed him.

"Alright, now to record your flight speed. Follow me," Dr. Anna spoke, breaking my thoughts.

Is she insane?? I can barely stand, much less fly!

I got off the table and followed her out of the room. A crew of soldiers met us as an escort.

I kept an eye on my surroundings, trying to memorize the layout. But escape really was looking impossible.

We walked into a large airplane hanger. It was the training facility. Looking around, I saw soldiers and officers working on various training contraptions or doing drills.

"Will, we're gonna use a wind simulator to test your flying and get an analysis on it."

I nodded, but really didn't care. I was infatuated with what was going on around me. But people were beginning to become infatuated with what was going on around them too. The stares I knew were headed my way hit me harder than expected. Now everything was an awkward staring contest.

I was led to a huge tunnel with a ridiculous fan thingy at the end.

"Will!" I heard my name echo.

I turned and saw Reece coming towards me.

"Ford! Back to your station!"

The soldier had a fire light in his eyes, but he closed them and exhaled.

"They're gonna have you fly, right? I wanna watch."

He winked and turned back to his officer who stared

oblivion into him.

I sighed as he left.

So much for that reunion.

When I heard a whirr I looked at the tunnel and saw the fan at the end begin to turn.

"Please step inside, Will," Dr. Anna said as she held open a door.

Hesitantly, I went inside and watched as the door was shut behind me.

I looked at Dr. Anna who stood behind a glass window, notepad and pen ready.

Behind me, I saw a vent that I guessed filtered the air outside.

At least I get to fly, though, … if I can.

Looking back to the window, I saw more spectators gathering. Among them was Reece.

Fan-friggin-tastic.

Once the air current was sturdy enough, I took off into an unsteady soar, my body was so not ready for this. The wind picked up and I went harder. I found myself at a flying sprint far beyond what I was in typical condition to do. And I paid the price. My wing started in a throb, which exploded into a fiery pain that made me want to curl in on myself. I teetered back down trying to land, but the wind was still going strong.

Cut the frickin' wind! I can't land!

I wasn't sure how it happened, but my wings caught, and I was thrown back. The pavement beneath me was nice and let me off with only a nearly smashed nose and a few skid marks on my elbows and knees. Finally, the fan began to slow down, and I looked up from the ground panting and sweating. I heard the entrance lift and footsteps come near me.

"That was TOTALLY wicked!!!!!!" Reece shouted in my ear.

"Could you not scream in my ear… please?"

"But you were flying faster than a jet or something!"

I thought about that comment before replying with a superstitious hum and said, "I don't think that's quite accurate, since I just got screwed by fake wind."

"FORD!"

Reece let go of me after we both heard his commander yell at him, this time a little less nicely than the first.

I took a step and to my horror, my legs gave out.

"Did you just fall?" Reece asked.

"NO!" I retorted, embarrassed. "I attacked the floor."

"Backwards?"

"Ever heard of talent??"

Reece laughs as he helped me up again.

"I better go before I get yelled at again. Later, Will."

I waved goodbye, successfully standing up this time.

"We have one more test, then we'll be done," Dr. Anna informed me. "Then you can return to your holding quarter."

Once again, Dr. Anna and her two subordinates whisked me away down a concrete hallway. The white lighting made it look eerie. The longer we walked the more I began to become worried as I sensed the atmosphere change. My gut was telling me that something was wrong, but what could I do about it?

We stopped in front of a room and Dr. Anna led me inside. It resembled a recording room for music except there was no mic. There was a desk with blinking lights and buttons.

I was pushed towards the entrance to the glass room as a few scientists filed in and began taking seats.

Where did they even come from??

"Wha-" I was cut off when the door shut.

I found myself alone, looking through the glass at the white coats who sat on the other side of the glass.

I pounded on the glass, "What is this?!"

The hair on the back of my neck stood up and goosebumps spread all over my skin. I felt the air become pressurized. Suddenly, I recognized it. Static.

Electricity! NO!!

I beat the glass frantically, trying to get them to let me out. But the pressure got worse.

Why? I asked before it happened. Why this?

Suddenly, a green light lit up in the corner and it began.

The electricity struck me again and I doubled over. This had been continuous. My yelling turned to screams, yelps, and finally muffled cries.

Why? What was the point?

"Absolute threshold…" Dr. Anna's voice echoed in my head.

My body shook as another bolt of electric current passed through my body. I never wondered what it'd feel like to be hit by lightning, but now I had the answer. It hurt. Another hit landed, I opened my mouth, but nothing came out. My voice was gone, replaced with a hoarse rasp. Again and again, they came.

Was there no end? Were they going to kill me now? I thought as tears rolled down my cheeks. I fell against the glass window and slid down.

If they did kill me, at least it would all be over. But did I really want that?

I pressed my balled fist against the glass.

"Stop," my voice betrayed me.

Another shock. I should've known, they had no intention of letting me off the hook that easy.

I fell to the floor and laid there struggling to breathe.

This is where I'll die.

I slipped in and out of consciousness. Only my coughing making me hang on.

Then, much to my relief, the room and scientists, even the pain disappeared. I heard static air crackling, then silence. Everything was perfect now.

CHAPTER 4

I HATE PERFECT THINGS

"He's still alive isn't he?" a voice asked in the distance.

"Yes ma'am, it's a temporary coma."

"Ah."

"He should be able to hear though, ma'am."

"Will?" I heard Dr. Anna's voice become louder. "Will, can you hear me?"

I could hear her, but I couldn't answer, and it's not like I wanted to either.

More silence, then a click.

I don't know how long I lay there, but I'd have been fine if it lasted forever. I had nothing to look forward to anyways.

Click.

There was a voice that swore.

"No, no, no, no, come on buddy, wake up!"

Who was this?

"Will, come on buddy!!!"

Reece.

"I put cards in my pocket…" he began. "…But I don't really want to play solitaire."

I gradually began to feel something on my chest. It was a hand.

"So please wake up."

My eyes opened and I saw a blurry Reece.

Along with feeling, the pain returned and in full force.

"Will! My gosh! You're gonna be okay now; you're okay," he comforted as my face twisted in pain.

Reece got to his feet in a squat and picked me up.

As we went out the door and back down the creepy hallway, I was happy. Why had I thought I was alone? Reece was here. I closed my eyes.

I had a friend.

When I woke up, I was in my cell on the bed jutting out from the wall.

Exhaling, I rolled over and sunk into the stiff padding acting as a mattress.

"How are you feeling?" I opened my eyes and saw Reece sitting against the glass.

Had he been here the entire time?

"My brain might be a little fried, but I'm okay," I said.

Reece smiled.

"I love that a pun is the first thing you say."

I shrugged.

"Rest up. I'll try to come by a little later."

I nodded, "Don't forget the cards we could have a few rounds of go fish."

"Don't worry," he said, opening the door. "I won't."

The door closed after him and I closed my eyes. Hadn't I already lost enough? Now what was I gonna do if the opportunity to escape arose? Would I just leave him?

The thoughts lingered in my mind before an answer finally came to me.

Yes.

I awoke with a jump. All the lights were off, and I was alone. The dream of the electric bolts came back to haunt my memories. My bed was cold like granite. I exhaled and rolled over, still disturbed by the dream. Fortunately, the pain from yesterday had been replaced with sore muscles. After a moment, I got up and walked over to the wall.

I guess Reece couldn't come and play cards. I sighed and leaned against the door panel.

My eyes flew open, and I jumped away.

Did the door just move?

The little angel on my shoulder began dancing and the demon on the other began punching his fist into his palm.

Pushing the door a little more, I stuck my head out and looked around. The soldiers outside sat in two chairs with their chins to their chests.

Wow, top notch security.

I stepped out. My eyes immediately searched for any tracking devices that might be on me but found none. The hallway that Dr Anna had led me through yesterday was dark.

This is odd, the door unlocked, soldiers asleep, and no one around.

Well, if they didn't want me out, it's their fault for leaving me unsupervised. Besides, who forgets to lock the freakin' door?

I tiptoed down the hallway and came to an opening. It had multiple passages that were all identical.

Crap to the eleventh power!

I chose the left one and followed it until it led me to a flight of stairs.

"I don't have time for this," I whispered as I started a silent ascent up the stairs. At the top, I saw a long hallway with more doors but with the blessing of labels. I walked by them all, scanning. One might lead to the outside. At the end of the hall I came to two glass doors and a balcony.

This is too perfect, my gut warned, you shouldn't go out there. Ignoring myself, I opened the door a little and saw a conjoining door to the platform that had been left open.

Hearing voices, I hid myself behind a wall.

"We need to train him," a male voice said roughly.

"Put him with the cadets," I recognized Dr Anna's voice. "If he refuses then we can use some disciplinary metho-."

"No," the male voice cut her off. "Put him with Ford. The cadet seems to have a connection with Ascella."

My brows furrowed.

"After this, assign him to Ford. Where is he by the way?"

"He's here."

I stopped breathing.

"Good, and it's working properly?"

"Yes, sir."

What on earth were they talking about?

I waited a few minutes before peeking behind the corner. It was clear now, and the two were gone.

Finally.

"Ascella."

If I'd been a cat, I would've jumped ten feet in the air and dug my claws into the ceiling. Whipping my head around, I saw a few soldiers.

Just great.

The soldier moved his hand to his gun on his belt and hovered it there. I took a step back and slowly unfurled my wings.

I watched the soldier put his hand on the gun and slide a small portion of it out.

"I wouldn't do that if I were you."

I raised an eyebrow, "I definitely think that you would. I jumped over the balcony as I heard gunshots and a radio. Lights began flooding the base.

Shoot, this place is big.

I pushed my wings past the soreness and into a glide. My speed began to dwindle. I can't keep this up.

Thunder rumbled in the distance. Absolutely fantastic; rain always made it hard to fly. I approached the border of the base with a relieved grin.

Too perfect. My head warned me, but I didn't care. I crossed it and felt a sharp sting on my arm. Was I being paranoid or was that coincidental? The sting gradually increased the further I got. I wasn't more than maybe two hundred feet when the sting turned into a full-blown shock.

"GGGAAAAaaaaHHHH!"

I yanked up my sleeve and saw nothing at first. Then I was shocked again, only this time, with a higher voltage. Everything locked up and gave out at once. I was lucky I hadn't been very high otherwise my crash land might've killed me.

The pain in my arm began to get more intense. The shocks became successive at a quicker pace.

This was all a trick, I thought. Whatever is on my arm or in it. I hadn't even been close to escaping.

I snapped out of my thoughts when I heard something.

My blood froze when movement came from behind me.

"Sorry kid," a gruff voice said. "But we had to make sure it worked."

"What are you talking about?" I grunted.

The man pulled out what looked like a bulky phone. It had a screen displaying my exact location via a blinking light. I laughed and nearly cried at the same time.

"Just put me to sleep," I growled.

"I've no orders to-"

"Please... just this one thing."

The man sighed. "Okay," he said finally. "Let's keep this

between you and me."

I nodded as he pulled out a syringe.

"Just make our fight sound cool."

The man looked at me in sympathy before injecting my arm.

"Don't worry kid, it will be."

"You know, I'm surprised I haven't become immune to this stuff," I mumbled, closing my eyes. The man put away the syringe.

"Me too."

I really do hate perfect things.

CHAPTER 5

DOG COLLARS AND KAWASAKIS

I woke up in a truck.

"He's awake," I heard.

I looked to the side to see stone-faced soldiers sitting against the wall looking at me.

Oh yippie, I'm not tied up.

Sitting up, I saw my predicament.

"Try anything stupid or we'll use that," said a man jabbing a finger at my neck.

I reached up and touched a sleek collar on my neck.

"What's this?" I asked, narrowing my eyes.

"A shock collar."

"Oh goodie! The chip in my arm isn't enough?"

The soldier scoffed, "The chip in your arm only works outside the base. That is so you don't act up on the inside."

Wow, I just couldn't love these people more.

When the vehicle stopped, I got out of the truck with the soldiers. From there, I was led inside and into an office.

The person I did not miss sat behind the desk.

"Hello, Will," Dr. Anna greeted me as she continued her paperwork. "Have a good time last night? Well, I hope you did cause that's the last of it. We're going to be swearing you in."

Wow, I'm soooo excited.

"We're assigning you with Ford, and if you try to leave, we'll find you."

I have a tracking chip and a shock collar on, you think I couldn't figure that out?

"As of today, you're gonna start training, and you will

keep that on till we can trust you."

She put her pen down and glared at me. "That collar on your neck is waterproof, hack-proof, you-proof, and everything else. It's not gonna come off so don't even try. However, if you want it off, then follow orders, don't complain, and behave."

I nodded at her, uncomfortable in her irritated gaze.

"I'm glad you understand; now, we'll move you into Cadet Ford's quarters, and you'll go straight to training. Your training will be different from the others since you're special."

I waited for her to say more but she didn't until she released a disturbing,

"You're dismissed."

I stood up and walked to the door, terrified.

Outside, I exhaled and took the uniform handed to me.

What the heck just happened? I am trapped but free all at the same time.

Once I'd changed, the soldiers escorted me to the many identical buildings which I assumed were the barracks. Reece was already waiting outside.

He looked me up and down and then at the soldiers accompanying me.

"I got him. Thanks though."

One of the soldiers stepped up to Reece and gave him a black thing.

"Keep this on you," he commanded. "At all times."

Reece exchanged a salute with the others and then we were alone.

"So I guess I'm supposed to train you, and my officer told me to see what you're like with a gun."

"Hold on, I was a prisoner and now I'm holding a gun?"

He shrugged and then a mischievous smile spread across his face.

"I have an idea."

"Okayy…" I trailed off remembering Dr. Anna's threat. "If we get in trouble and I die…"

"Oh you're gonna be fine."

Reece motioned for me to follow him, and I did.

"What's this idea?" I asked.

Reece softly chuckled, "You'll love it, trust me."

Love it? Sure, I'll love how this idea will be the reason I'll be killed.

I realized we were headed for a larger complex building that had a gigantic skylight. As we walked inside, the first things I saw were a line of neatly parked black vehicles and Kawasaki sportbikes. But my attention was grabbed by the trees, vines, rocks, and dirt that took up half of the building. It was some kind of man-made forest.

"What's this?" I asked, pointing to the faux forest that was just casually inside the building.

"It's one of the terrain simulators. We've got four and this is the jungle one."

"I'm sorry, what?"

"We're gonna have a competition on who's the better marksman."

Yup, I'm gonna die.

"Ever shot a gun before?" Reece asked me and raised his eyebrows.

"Well yeah, but-"

"Wonderful! I'll get a bike, and you'll fly. We'll take the easy trail so don't worry."

I stared at Reece.

HUH?

I watched him take a bike and walk it over to the opening of a narrow dirt path.

Unfurling my wings, I came over to him. "Wait, so why does the government have an indoor forest?"

"Here," Reece said as he handed me a shotgun. "Also here's another strip of ammunition. There are twenty-four targets on this course, and they blink green. Think of it as laser tag or airsoft, but with a real gun."

"But with a REAL gun," I mocked. "I know how to shoot a gun and are you just going to ignore my question?"

"Yes."

It'd been nearly a year since I'd shot a gun at all, and there was no way this was going to end well.

I stepped up to the dirt path, and Reece kicked the stand up with a roar of the engine.

"Marks, get set, GO!"

I took off into a sprint, then a low soar. I looked at the gun. It showed red.

"Red you're dead," my dad's voice echoed.

I heard the first shot and saw Reece had already hit a target.

What the- how?!

A blinking light caught my eye, and below it, the round target. I aimed my gun and pulled the trigger. The recoil was terrible. My arms jerked back, and the shot went way off into the bushes.

I glanced at Reece who was laughing his butt off and zoomed ahead.

You know what, frick you!!

I pushed to increase my own speed, playing catch up while searching frantically for another blinking light. There was a cloud of dust from the motorcycle up ahead and wondered what Reece had done now. I looked above it and saw the walls meet.

Oh...

Tucking my wings, I spun changing directions. After only five more minutes and a few missed targets, I came up at the end of the trail. Reece's face lit up when he saw me.

"Finally!" he said as I'd landed. "I'd begun to think you'd accidentally shot yourself or something."

I gave him a dirty look.

"I haven't shot a freakin' gun since last year and certainly not while flying." Reece threw his head back and laughed. "Don't worry, we'll fix that. I'm a pretty confident shooter so I'll teach you."

Okay, A-hole.

"That's just great. I can't wait to watch you laugh at me some more," I spat.

"Okay, if you'd seen yourself shooting, you would've laughed too, Toothpick."

"Toothpick!?"

Reece bent over laughing as I rationalized whether I should slug him or not.

"We'll go to the range and get you back into the swing of it before we getcha flying."

"Now?"

"Well yeah, unless you wanna try the bike out or something."

I hesitated, giving Reece an opening to decide for me.

"Get on."

"What? No! I can't steer that thing."

"Just get on Will, it's easier than you think."

This guy had more hope in me than he should've.

I swung my leg over while saying a quick prayer, and

Reece put two helmets on our heads before settling in behind me.

"ONWARD!!" he shouted like a dork.

I swear, he must be trying to kill me.

I cranked my heel backward and gripped the handles tight for my life as the bike sped off.

After the range, Reece was paged by Dr. Anna.

It was random, which kinda scared me, but nonetheless, we both stood outside looking at her door.

"I'll be out here when you're done," Reece said.

"Thanks," I grimaced, then walked into the office I dreaded so much.

"Will…" Dr. Anna's voice trailed off, and I watched her eyes soak in all my cuts and bruises before she started again. "I was monitoring your location and saw that earlier you got a little too far from Ford. I'm warning you, the second time that happens…" she motioned to my shock collar, "It's not gonna be good for you."

I nodded and looked at my feet.

"Permission to speak."

"Granted."

"Can I ask you a question?"

I gained Dr. Anna's attention briefly, but then she went back to her papers.

"Depends on what it is," she said absentmindedly.

"How'd you kill them?"

Anna froze looking at her paperwork.

"Who, Will?"

"My parents."

There was a long silence that passed between us before she answered.

"I could answer that, but I won't… for your sake."

My brows furrowed. What they did was so bad they won't tell me.

"Here."

I looked up to see Dr. Anna lay a feather on her desk. I recognized it.

"How did you…" I trailed off.

Dr. Anna shook her head.

"You're dismissed."

"But-"

"You're dismissed, Ascella," she repeated sternly.

After giving her a long look, I turned and left.

"Hey! How'd it go?" Reece greeted me.

I don't know what gave it away, but Reece's smile quickly turned to a frown when he saw me. He left me in silence for the majority of the way back, which I appreciated; I wouldn't have been able to carry on a conversation anyways.

"What happened?" he tried once we'd started up the stairs to our room.

"Nothing," I muttered.

"Will… please tell me what's wrong."

I was sick to my stomach thinking about it, so I pulled out my father's feather and held it for him to see.

"My dad…" My voice cracked.

Reece opened the door, remaining silent until I laid down on my bed.

"I'm sorry," he finally said. "It's hard to lose someone like that."

I wanted to laugh. This guy had absolutely no clue as to how torn up this made me.

"I lost both of my parents in one day, my freedom, my

old life," I whispered. "Now I'm alone and everything that I thought I would have forever is gone."

"I'm here though."

"Yeah, you are because you're on the side that shot the guns, not the side slaughtered by them," I snapped.

Reece didn't respond.

I clutched the feather in my hand. My mind was filled with flashbacks of that day. I wanted to cry again, but I couldn't. I'd already begun filing everything away to be forgotten. Maybe if I slept, I'd forget it all.

Sleep. That sounded like the best route of escape.

CHAPTER 6

SO I GUESS I'M ANAKIN NOW

I lowered my hand as I finished my oath.

"Congratulations, Ascella, you're an official soldier now."

I saluted the lieutenant as he handed me a uniform with my last name printed on it.

The last few months had been rough, but I'd been comforted by the hope that I could trade my service for freedom.

I was dismissed with Reece and the others who'd witnessed the informal swearing.

Reece stared at the ground as we began to file.

"Hey Will."

"Hey?"

"I got a question for ya."

"Okay."

"When's your birthday?"

"On the day I was born."

"Oh my go...Why are you like this!!"

I sighed, "We've been over this Reece, and my answer remains the same."

"Okay okay fine, I won't do anything. Now, will you tell me?"

"Surely, you don't think I'm that stupid."

Reece threw his head back and groaned.

"Fine!"

We walked to the range, or more like Reece followed me, his stupid, freckled face grinning all the way.

I'd checked myself in and began shooting when Reece spoke again.

"I'm gonna get John to look it up."

"What? No!!" I said pausing my fire, "and who is John?"

"He's a friend of mine, real geeky and smart, like Tony Stark but that guy will never get a Pepper Potts. I'll just ask him to get into the system and look up your information."

"Absolutely not."

"You can't stop me."

I could if I killed you, I wanted to say but I decided to go with a different approach, one that didn't involve murder.

"Please don't."

Reece looked at me and hesitated.

"You're awful at guilt-tripping. I'm definitely asking him now."

I rolled my eyes, irritated at his persistence about the matter.

"Just leave me alone. I need to train for the assessment tonight."

Reece was about to start talking, but I quickly avoided it by continuing my rounds.

"Will, you're a natural, you'll be fine."

"Easy for you to say," I grumbled. "This is like what, the fiftieth time for you?"

"Okay, I get your point, but I was sworn in nearly three years ago!"

I snorted and put my pistol down.

"Is it time yet?"

"No, thirty more minutes before it starts."

"Sounds like enough time for a little competition then."

"Oh no…. What're you thinking?" Reece asked, the corners of his lips curling.

After turning my gun back into the clerk, I led the way into the gym. Going over to the rack of gear, I pulled some athletic wrap.

Tossing one to Reece, I flashed a smile at him and began wrapping my hands.

"I've been learning to get my wings involved in some hand to hand, so let's test it out."

"Ahh, the Padawan challenging the Jedi master? You sure that's wise, Anakin?"

I smirked once Reece joined me on the boxing mat. "I'm Anakin now?"

"I'm gonna think teaching you was a waste of time if you don't win," he joked.

My eyes narrowed. "You've already lost, idiot."

Reece rubbed his jaw and gave me a dirty look as we listened to the positions of the assessment.

The assessment didn't seem too hard. If I understood everything the sergeant was saying, it was a simple plan, get from point A to point B. I was put on the defense team that was broken up into five divisions. Our job was to drive five trucks, one for each division, along a road in a terrain simulator. The goal was to prevent our trucks from getting captured or destroyed by the five attack divisions. The sergeant finished explaining and called out what divisions we were a part of.

Getting up, I searched for the team I was put in. Unfortunately, Reece and I had been separated. He'd been put on the attacking team.

I found the group with the letter A etched into the back of their vests. I began walking over to them.

If I understood right, Rank A was the front defense

group.

"Ascella," I heard the leading officer say to me.

"Sir!" I responded.

"I know you're close friends with Ford, but don't let that make you hesitate. We're going to have you be our eyes in the sky. Here, take this radio with you, and let me know when you see enemy teams."

I nodded.

"And Ascella,"

"Sir?"

"Use channel 3 and don't get shot."

I smiled at my officer. I kinda liked him.

A boom caught my attention, and I saw the doors opening up. Five large cargo trucks stood ready to go. The defense team drivers began to get into them.

So all we have to do is get those across to the other side without taking high casualties, seems easy enough.

The roar of jeeps took my attention away from the trucks. My leading officer got in one with the rest of my comrades.

We're starting.

"Will!"

I made eye contact with my rank leader.

"What're you doing? Get with the scouts!"

I gave him a sharp nod and unfurled my wings. Taking off, I struggled to pass the first truck and get to the scouts riding on motorcycles in the front.

As I scanned the ground, I caught sight of the scouts leaving their bikes and taking positions in the trees.

Once they'd disappeared, I gained altitude. The stillness down below was disturbed by the faint rumbling of the trucks and the blinking targets on the vests of the ranks.

A minuscule light beam lit up beside me.

What the… Surely there is no way they can see me.

I followed the direction it had come and noticed the small group speeding towards the line of trucks.

"Eyes in the Sky to Command, enemy sighted twelve o'clock!" I spoke on the radio.

"Command acknowledged."

Seconds later, a light show exploded down below.

"Command to Eyes in the Sky, come down!" my radio alerted me.

Frick yeah! Time to go kick someone's butt!

I tucked my wings and dove down to the battle. Swooping in, I settled onto a branch and began playing sniper. One at a time, I turned blinking green lights on the enemy vests to red. I'd almost picked off an entire group before they figured me out and started shooting back.

As I tried to dodge the lasers being shot, my foot slipped off the branch and I fell.

"Get him!" one of the enemies yelled.

NOPE.

I wanted to stop and grab my gun I dropped, but I didn't have time. I sprinted off into the trees.

The terrain was dense and made it hard for a quick getaway. But if I was having this much trouble surely my pursuers would too.

I stopped behind a tree and tried to catch my breath as quietly as I could. Looking up, I realized how disadvantaged I was. The trees would make it impossible to fly out of here.

Dang, am I supposed to fight them?

"All combat to the front. All combat to the front." My radio went off loudly.

I quickly turned it off, but it was too late. They'd found

me.

The group of four had me surrounded with their guns pointed at me.

"Can we just talk about it?" I tried.

I got a laugh from one of them, but the rest stared at me apathetically.

"I really don't want to fight you guys, ya know."

"Neither do we, Ascella."

He pulled the trigger, and I jumped to the side, narrowly dodging it. I sized up my opponents before targeting the first one.

Here we go.

I met the closest one with my fist and ripped the gun from his hands. The others shot their lasers, and I used the guy as a shield. His vest turned red, and I dropped him to take on the other one that charged me. I blocked his punches and drove my knee between his legs. He screamed and crumbled holding his crotch. The third shot at me, and I threw myself back to avoid it. I succeeded in my back handspring and charged the guy. I needed to take care of him before the other dude recovered. I gripped his arm and felt my energy spike. Gritting my teeth, I took the fourth out by throwing the guy I held into him. A laser beam narrowly missed my vest and went past me.

Dang, he'd recovered.

My eyes narrowed, and I unfurled my wings. The other two got up and charged me at the same time. Jumping and propelling myself up with my wings, I dodged them.

Do it now.

I landed and threw my fist into the left guy's face. Suddenly, there was a hand on my ankle pulling my leg out from under me. I hadn't even registered the pain from the three punches when I was hoisted up by my collar and pressed against a tree trunk.

Shoot.

A pistol was pressed up against my vest as the eyes of the soldier peered into mine.

"I'm impressed. You took three of us down, but you still got a long way to go."

I smirked. "Don't underestimate me."

"Oh, I'm not."

"Yeah, you are."

I pulled the trigger of the gun I'd taken from one of the "dead" guys, and his vest lights turned red.

The soldier stumbled back.

"How did you…"

"Pay more attention next time!" I called, replacing the pistol back into my vest. I sprinted back the way I'd come and turned on my radio.

The things I heard weren't good. My group was in trouble.

I took flight once I'd reached the road. The trucks were way ahead, but the glow of lights directed me to where I needed to be.

Suddenly, my radio came on.

"Command to Ascella! Where are you!?"

"Ran into trouble, coming!" I radioed back.

"Hurry!"

I forced myself to fly faster towards the action. Finally, they were in sight, but what I saw made my skin crawl. There was someone on the roof of a truck taking out my comrades. The lone soldier was headed towards the first truck. My comrades began calling to me to land. The soldier looked back at me, and I immediately recognized him. It was Reece.

He started charging for where I'd begun to land.

My feet hit the vehicle's roof and at the same time my mind screamed at me to turn around.

I spun, dodging the laser shot by him.

Reece was surprised.

Folding my wings, I dropped and rolled on the truck just in time to dodge the punch Reece threw at me.

"Fancy meeting you here!" he shouted as he threw another punch.

"Much obliged, good sir!" I yelled, swinging an uppercut that he blocked. He hooked and I blocked. He tried to use his elbow, and I threw my head back to dodge it.

The punches thrown back and forth got old. Knowing this, Reece began to use an occasional laser or two. After I watched his movements, I saw the opening I'd been looking for.

Too risky! My head screamed.

But I ignored myself. Reece was in a perfect position.

I jumped and opened my wings as I propelled myself into him. I swung my legs over his shoulder while using my arm to hook his neck. My momentum pulled us both forward and off the back of the moving truck. When we hit the ground, it was over.

"I hate you..." Reece coughed.

I smiled as I pulled out the pistol and shot his vest. The lights on his vest went red, pronouncing Reece "dead."

I helped Reece to his feet as he stared at me.

"Where'd you even learn a move like that?"

I smiled even bigger, happy with my accomplishment. "Oh, I don't know. Maybe I noticed a small opening in your defense a long time ago, and it just took me a while to figure out how to take advantage of it."

"And you never told me?" he huffed. "You suck."

I laughed, then turned and flew off to catch up to the line of trucks that had left during my battle with Reece.

I caught sight of the trucks nearing the other side of the terrain. Excitement filled me; we were winning!!

Seconds later, one of the trucks at the back stopped moving and fell behind.

My eyes narrowed as I dove down to it to check out the problem.

I saw the driver sitting in the seat behind the wheel with a red-lighted vest. He'd been shot. Immediately, I scoured the trees and greenery for hidden snipers.

I opened the door.

"Move over."

I heard the driver scoot, and I got in and started the truck back up. I pressed the gas and gripped the wheel as I continued to scan the trees as I drove to catch back up.

Good thing, there were no cops around cause I definitely did not have my driver's license.

I cruised along until I saw the rear of another truck. Something flashed.

"DUCK!" I yelled as I took my own advice to avoid a light beam that shone through the window.

I sat back up and pulled my pistol out to shoot back in the direction that the beam came from.

My radio went off suddenly with a voice.

"Command to all units, terrain boundary in five hundred feet. Terrain boundary in five hundred feet."

I heard a thud on the top of the truck and assumed it was someone from an enemy squad.

Great.

"Take the wheel," I told the previous driver.

"I'm dead," he reminded me pointing to the red light on his vest.

Gah, useless!! I wanted to yell.

Looking ahead, I saw the closest truck to us and looked around for some sort of tool.

"Is there anything in here that can connect us to them?"

"There are a pair of hooks in the console."

I opened it and grabbed the hooks the driver told me about.

"Okay," I breathed. "Here goes nothing."

Accelerating the vehicle before I slipped out of the door gave me the chance to let it roll along with the other trucks for a split second. Taking the narrow loophole, I connected the two trucks together with the hooks before turning to the top of the vehicle I had been driving. There were two soldiers from Squad 5 on top planting something.

Oh heck no!

They saw me right as I tackled one of them off the roof of the truck and to the ground. He was stunned by the football move, giving me a second to shoot him before I got up. I spun on my heel and took off after the other guy.

I sprinted and grabbed onto the back of the truck. After scaling it, I pulled myself up enough to aim my gun at the other guy who jumped down and darted off. Getting onto the truck, I saw the bomb.

In a panic, I sprinted over and saw the seconds counting down.

3 …

Immediately, I dug into it, pulling apart the wires.

2 …

My eyes widened in horror. We'd fail the mission if this went off. Then I did the only thing I knew to do and took off the panel the bomb was on to propel myself into the air.

A high-pitched siren went off announcing the end of the simulation.

I exhaled.

Did we win?

Below me, the trucks were past the boundary line. All of them in one piece.

I landed and dropped the panel with the bomb still attached to it.

I sunk to the ground panting. The vehicle continued to roll forward until it went through an opening into a large hanger where people began filing out and meeting in the middle to see the results that were displayed on the big screen.

I sat up.

"Hey Will!" I heard a familiar voice yell at me. "Come check out your results!"

I saw Reece standing with another guy and girl. Looking at the point system, I saw all the kills and saves. Then I saw my results.

"The frick…?" I muttered under my breath.

CHAPTER 7

NATURE WOULD'VE LOVED ME, BUT I RESISTED

After seeing the scores, we were all called to be evaluated by the Analyzers, one by one.

"Reece Ford!" a voice yelled out.

Reece gave me a wink before walking behind a door and disappearing.

This was like the waiting room in a doctor's office, I thought as I looked around at the nervous soldiers lined up after me.

"Hey," a voice across from me said.

Looking up, I made eye contact with a female that sent my head into all sorts of confusion. She was pretty and talking to me; something didn't add up.

"Hey?" I replied.

She laughed, and she took my reply as an invitation to talk.

"You're Will, right? Reece was talking about you during training."

Oh no.

I grunted in response and glanced at her eyes quickly before looking at the ground. Man, was she pretty.

"My name's Elizabeth, but everyone calls me 'Liz.'"

I was thankful for whatever reason made her talk to me. This was too good to be true.

I smiled at the nickname and nodded at her.

"Is Will short for something too?"

Wait, how do I talk to girls again?

My mind blanked so I shook my head.

"Is it for William?"

I nodded again at her, and I heard her chuckle.

She's trying something; she has to be.

"You only ever talk to Reece don't you?"

I'm such an idiot! Someone kill me, please...

I felt the blush come to my face as she called me out.

"Sorry," I muttered. "I- I mean I-."

Dang, stuttering now of all times? I'm gonna stay single forever.

She nodded and leaned forwards a little.

Do I even know how to kiss someone? Surely she wouldn't do that now; we just met!

The panic sirens went off in my head until she stopped and spoke to me in a lowered tone.

"Nothing's wrong with that, just know that there are other people who wanna get to know you too."

I felt like a scared little animal she was trying to coax, but regardless I forced a smile.

"Will Ascella!" the stern voice called again. I jumped.

Gah, how embarrassing.

I stood up and waved shyly at Liz before walking into the room where I saw a round table

with four elderly people sitting.

"Will Ascella," the first one spoke. "It's a pleasure to get to meet you after hearing so much."

I nodded.

"So let's take a look at your results," another Analyzer said.

He clicked a few buttons, and a holographic screen appeared with recorded footage of me sparring with Reece.

"I must say that I've never seen a move like this, yet the wings, helping you with a moments cover, it turned out perfect. However, I must criticize some of the techniques here…"

As I listened to the praise and critiques, I wondered if this was all it was gonna be.

What was so special about getting top ten then?

The footage disappeared, and the faces of the analyzers peered at me until I was uncomfortable.

"Ascella, can we trust you?"

I was puzzled by the question.

Well, I'd hope so.

"Yes sir?" I said.

"You were in the top ten, but you're young and not fully human. You swore in this afternoon, so pardon me for doubting, but I can't trust you myself yet."

I sat there, silent.

What just happened…

"I have a question, sir," I spoke up. "If I may?"

"Go on."

"Why are you unable to trust me?"

The analyzer put his hands into a steeple and leaned back in his chair.

"To be straightforward, the top ten go on an amateur mission to get hands-on experience before we station them. That mission typically gives us tabs on what kind of soldier they are such as a combat leader, agent, IT, and so forth. Understand?"

I nodded, and he continued.

"This simulation gave me a little direction on what kind of a soldier you are, but with a mission I'd see it more clearly. But there's a problem; we've been told to look for specifics in you, and you haven't shown them. We're also not dangling freedom in front of you and expecting you to actually ignore it. On a mission, if you ran off it could be fatal to everyone else there."

The man paused before placing his elbows on the table.

"I don't know about the others, but I don't trust you."

I was stunned, and my eyes furrowed.

"Is there a possibility that I could get a mission anyways?"

"Yes, I was just telling you what the reason is, if you don't. However, again with the trust issue, I'm going to have to talk it out with some other officers and the general before we make a final decision. In the meantime, wait for an answer. You'll know by tonight."

I nodded and stood up with the Analyzers, saluted them, then dismissed myself.

The chilly air of the night met my skin as I walked to the barracks.

I thought about what the Analyzer had said.

I'll see the outside world again. If it's the last thing I do.

I glanced at the moon before I started up the staircase.

From the corner of my eye, I saw something move. I studied the area where the movement occurred. As much as I hated the idea of something unknown sneaking around, I hated the idea of me going to investigate it even more. That's how people in horror movies get killed.

"Whatever," I muttered under my breath.

I made my way up the staircase and walked into my room.

"Will!" I felt his bear hug before I heard Reece finish my name. "How'd it go?"

I smiled. "It was pretty good. They're still thinking about whether or not they'll let me go on the mission, but I'm keeping my hopes up."

Reece's green eyes stared at me bewildered.

"You know, if they let you go, this'll be our first combat mission in the field!"

I laughed with Reece as he punched my arm.

"Sorry, I'm just excited to go fight bad guys with you, bro!" he said.

I sighed and shook my head.

"Don't worry about it."

Reece's bright grin got brighter if it was even possible.

If he doesn't stop, I'm going to go blind.

"Oh yeah, before-"

There was a knock at the door.

We both turned and looked at it before looking at each other and then back to the door again.

Reece walked towards it and opened it.

"Hello?"

I heard a low hum of another voice

"Yeah, he's inside… oh, okay."

I listened to Reece before I heard him call my name.

"It's for you."

I nodded as I switched places with him. I saw a brown-haired man maybe only a year or two older than me.

"Yes?" I asked.

"I was sent to inform you that you'll be attending the mission briefing in the morning. Congrats, you've been accepted."

I've been what?

I thanked the man then closed the door as he turned to leave. I felt numb.

"That seemed like a good sign," Reece said.

"It was, I'm going."

Reece jumped up off his bed and engulfed me in another

hug again. If he'd squeezed any harder I might've blacked out.

"Dude. Let. Go." I rasped.

He released me and stepped back.

I saw the happiness on his face displayed without reserve.

He held out his fist and illuminated the room with his smile.

"Our first mission together…"

I nodded and bumped fists with him.

"Our first mission."

"Well then, get some sleep, Hot Shot. After the briefing, we'll probably leave tomorrow."

"What happens at the briefing?" I asked.

"From what I know, my dad told me that it just summarizes the goals and assigns you with your squads and such."

"Your dad is military?"

Reece nodded and pulled out his packed bag, "Ex-military."

I followed Reece's example and began packing what little things I had.

As I changed into my sleeping shorts and slid under the covers on my bed. My mind reflected on the day's events.

Suddenly, I chuckled.

"What's so funny?" Reece asked.

"You know what the Analyzers pulled up when they were talking to me?"

"What?" Reece asked me.

"The fight we had when I kicked your butt."

"Oh shut up!!" he spat while slamming the light switch. "That won't happen again."

"Bet."

"Go to sleep!"

I chuckled again as I got comfortable, then sleep came.

In my dream, I was out of breath.

I was running, my gasps echoing around me. What was I running from? The world around me was distorted but real.

The terrain beneath my feet melted into a wheat field and released terrifying sounds.

Something was following me, hidden by the grain. Looking ahead, two statues loomed over the top of a hill. Immediately, my instincts told me to hide. That was where safety from this thing that was chasing me lay. As I got closer, I realized the sculptures were of my parents.

I leaned against one trying to catch my breath. Suddenly, the silence stopped. What was that?

Taking another look from behind the statue, my ears were filled with the sound of locusts, though there wasn't one in the sky. I relaxed, hiding back behind the statue, but two yellow eyes bore into me. The scaley black hands gripped my neck, digging their talons into the sides of my neck.

I tried to scream but was lifted off my feet as the creature's slitted eyes narrowed at me in amusement. It's insect wings fluttered, and the statues of my parents came crashing down behind me. As I dangled, the ground beneath me fell away exposing a black hole leading to what my mind registered as Hell. The creature grinned at me, and to my horror it ripped the wings off my back letting them fall into the hell hole beneath me.

I tried to scream, yell, and call for help. But my voice

wouldn't work; I could barely breathe. The black creature's grip on my neck began to lighten as the body of the creature got more and more intangible. Then I was falling into the black hole of darkness.

I jumped and found myself back in reality. Sitting up, I wiped the sweat that was running down my brow.

"Glad you're awake. Were ya toasty or having a nightmare?"

I looked over to the side to see Reece, halfway dressed, bent over me.

I could always rely on him to make light of a situation. "Why didn't you wake me up?"

"I tried but you wouldn't respond so…"

"Sorry," I finally answered. "Guess I was just… tired."

Reece peered at me curiously, stepped away and finished getting into his uniform. I saw him pulling out his backpack and putting things in it. Then it dawned on me.

"What time is it?" I asked.

Reece paused and looked at his watch.

"Almost 5:30."

I rushed to get myself out of bed, and the sweat on my body began to get cold, giving me goosebumps.

"I'm friggin cold…" I grumbled.

"I wonder why, Sweaty."

I rolled my eyes at the new nickname and continued with my own business. After putting on my boots and pulling on my backpack, I felt like I'd forgotten something.

"Hey dude, have you seen my feather?"

"Yeah, they're all on your wings."

"I hate you," I muttered. "I meant my dad's feather."

I watched Reece laugh at himself. "Geez someone is grumpy this morning."

"No, you're just too smiley."

"Wow, what a comeback. Anyways, check that box over there."

I followed Reece's finger to the slender black box lying on the shelf on the wall.

As I walked over to it, Reece talked to me.

"I put it in there since we're traveling and all; hope you like it."

I opened the box and pulled the tissue paper aside.

"I wanted to do a little something special for ya so…."

I held up the chain that had my dad's white feather dangling at the bottom of it.

"I take back what I said about hating you."

"Apology accepted."

Setting the feather down, I turned around to face Reece with the biggest grin.

"Thank you." I said turning back to the box.

"It's a clip so you can…"

I looked at the metal base and saw what Reece was talking about. Unclipping it, I pulled out my dog tag and clipped it on.

"Thank you, Reece," I whispered while tucking the feather under my shirt.

"You're welcome, dude; but hey, I need to go see John this morning."

I nodded, "Okay."

Reece walked to the door then left.

I walked into the bathroom and looked in the mirror.

I can't believe it, I'm going straight to the mission.

While combing my hair, a knock at the door snapped me out of my thinking.

"Yes?"

Was Reece back already?

The knock sounded again.

I stood up, straightening my uniform and opened the door. There stood General Gray.

Huh?

I tried to hide the shock while my mind searched for every rule I'd broken in the past month. I saluted him and swallowed nervously.

"At ease, Ascella, this is unprofessional." The general waved as he gestured for entrance into the room.

I stepped aside and let the general walk in as I eyed him suspiciously.

Why is he here?

"I'm getting straight to the point since I'm limited on time."

"How exquisitely wonderful," I thought, as I sat across from him on my bed.

"I've changed my mind. I need to see something in you before I can send you off."

Hold on, what?

"I need you to earn your place out there."

Wonderful, what do you want me to do?! Make the half court shot?

Gray ended his statement and rested his elbows on his knees.

"Nobody is aware yet, and there's no harm telling you, but I'm pushing back the mission and setting up a simulation tonight. I'm going to give you another chance."

My gaze went to the floor then to my hands.

"Sir," I started, "what exactly are you expecting from me?"

"That is up to you, son."

Son? Oh no, don't you start calling me that.

"... but I'm out of time. The simulation will be announced at breakfast," Gray informed me as he stood up. "Excuse me."

The general saluted, and I did the same. I followed him to the door where he stood in the doorway for a moment before saying in a low tone, "Prove to me that you're your father's son."

The door shut, and the general was gone.

I stood there looking at the door dumbfounded.

What does he need? A blood test?

I turned and shook the confusion from my mind.

What is even going on anymore?

The door clicked and opened, and I saw a face I actually wanted to see.

"How'd your meeting with John go?" I asked.

"Great! Wanna go get breakfast?" Reece asked, smiling bright like always.

I followed him out and down the stairs when I heard Reece chuckle.

"What?" I asked curious.

"You know, John amazes me," Reece replied as he looked off into the distance.

"How so?"

"Well, he's developing this new program, and it's super cool!" Reece mused as we headed towards the cafeteria. "It's like a mix between Google home and bluetooth, but John's got it on his laptop, so he's making it compatible with his phone."

"Cool, but what's the point if it's just better bluetooth?"

"Well, you know Siri?"

"Yeah."

"It's like that, but it's got its own intelligence."

My eyebrow raised, "Has John always been able to tinker like this?"

"You know," Reece paused, "I guess he has. John and I were friends back in high school. He was a senior when I was a freshman, but in the classes we shared he was always fiddling with something."

I smiled at the ground as the memory of my dad doing the same thing passed through my mind.

"If I recall right," Reece continued, "John was the captain of the robotics team when they went to nationals."

"Seriously?"

"Mmmhmm."

Silence passed between us before I decided to share my morning's details.

"I got a visit this morning."

"By who?" he asked as he held the cafeteria door for me.

"General Gray."

I looked up at Reece to see him staring at me with his eyebrows scrunched.

"Why?"

"Well," I paused having second thoughts. "There's going to be a second simulation tonight."

"Okay? And?"

"The mission has been put on hold till then."

"Wait what? Why?"

"I don't know," I lied. "But he talked about it like it was a down low thing."

"But why did he only tell you that?"

Shoot!

"Well, that wasn't all…" I lowered my voice as we came

closer to people in the food line.

"Lemme guess, you have to take the second simulation."

"Yup."

Reece sat down across from me at the table in frustration.

"But you passed."

"I know, but Gray wanted to see something that he didn't during the first examination."

"But you passed."

"Yeah, and that doesn't matter. I've got to have his stamp of approval."

I picked at my pancakes as Reece aggressively chewed his eggs.

"So then what is he looking for, huh?"

"He wouldn't tell me."

"Liar."

I made eye contact with him.

"What do you mean?"

"Stop lying, you haven't given me full details since this conversation started."

Shoot! Shoot! Shoot! How did he know? What gave him the red flag?

"I just need to pass the simulation tonight and we're good."

Reece eyed me cautiously.

"I'll do it with you."

"You can't, it's only those who failed the first time."

"You're joking..."

"Do I look like a comedian?" I asked apathetically.

Reece and I just looked at each other.

"Didn't realize this was funny to you."

"It's not."

"Then why are you laughing?"

"I'm not."

"Stop lying."

"Shut up."

"I know you won't agree, but you are funny..."

"I'm not funny, just a mean guy who you think is joking."

Reece rolled his eyes and went back to his food.

I got the eerie feeling I was being watched. I turned and looked around before I saw them.

The two were snickered as they looked away.

"Hey Reece, who're they?" I asked him, sliding my eyes back in their direction.

"Who?"

"Four o'clock, male blond and brunette."

Reece looked and did a double glance before groaning.

"Just ignore them."

"Why?"

"Cause nobody likes those two, so just ignore them."

I looked back then followed Reece's instructions.

We stood up with our empty plates and dropped them off to be cleaned. Suddenly, the intercom echoed through the facility.

"Attention all cadets! Those who did not pass the simulation mission, report to Warehouse 1B by 10:30..." The message repeated before shutting off abruptly.

"Guess that'd be me."

"I'm coming with you."

"You have drill don't you?" I said.

Reece rubbed the back of his neck and looked at the floor.

"It got cancelled?"

"Uh huh, sure."

"Fine! I'll be there in spirit though."

"I'll take that."

"But you better hurry."

As I looked at the clock, a four-letter word blared in my mind. I spun on my heel and ran. I could hear Reeece's laughter behind me. I wasn't about to be late. I took off into a low soar to the warehouse to make it five minutes before I was supposed to be there.

Barreling through the doors, I ran into the sea of cadets. I turned, which made my wing clip someone's shoulder.

"Watch it, Ascella."

Great, I thought as I looked at the blond and brunette from breakfast.

"Haha, my bad," I attempted.

The last thing I need is a fight with these guys.

The brunette raised an eyebrow as he sized me up.

"Yeah, it is," the blond sassed me.

I was taken back by the cold response.

"Okay…" I mumbled as they turned and walked away.

"Hey Freak!"

I stopped, knowing who the slur was thrown at.

I glanced behind me to see the same two making their way through the crowd back towards me.

"Name's Trevor," the blond introduced.

"Austin," the brunette grunted with less entitlement.

"Let's be friends," Trevor feigned a grin while gripping my shoulder.

My conscience begged me to tear this kid to shreds.

Just kill him.

No.

All you have to do is take him to a good height 'accidentally' drop him then 'splat.' Snuff out his miserable little life.

No.

You're helping the environment!!

NO. Now shut the frick up!

I snapped back to reality and realized I hadn't responded to this "threat-posal."

"Yeah, sure."

The grip tightened, making me wince.

"Listen little bird, don't make me angry because I'll break that pride of yours."

I might've been intimidated if I wasn't still stumped by his nickname.

'Little Bird'? He's wrong there because I could go head to head with Big Bird from Sesame Street.

"Ford ain't here to protect you, so I suggest you better learn the ropes."

"Okay."

I received Austin's final threat before they went on their way.

I rolled my eyes as they disappeared within the sea of people.

What a load of crap.

But their words echoed through my head. I wasn't a freak, I was human... mostly human. I was interrupted by the closing doors and an air of attention that washed over the room. As I peered ahead, I noticed the others forming lines like someone was coming through. Suddenly, the people in front of me stepped aside to let an officer passing out orange keys come through.

I was handed one and looked it over, then I wasn't sure which was worse, being called a freak or getting special treatment.

A shout of attention boomed from a sergeant who stood at the front and saluted General Gray as he walked into the warehouse.

Gray stood for a moment before putting us at ease.

"There's going to be a simulation tonight for you all. I am giving you this free day to prepare and train. Meet in this warehouse no later than nine. If you're late you automatically fail. From here, you'll be directed to the locker bay to get the gear we have approved. There will be a short orientation on the simulation and weapons. You may not take a gun aside from the selection given to you. That is all, you're dismissed."

He left me with mixed emotions. I wasn't sure to be relieved or terrified. Exiting the building, I looked at the key I was given.

This is probably to the locker bay. Interesting way to do it, Gray.

My nervousness from this morning resurrected even stronger. I had to remember Gray was good at this, I needed to meet his expectations which was impossible in my opinion, but that was fine. I'd play his game.

CHAPTER 8

I GIVE PANCAKES AND RECEIVE CREPES

The simulation was in half an hour, and I found myself alone in the gear bay thinking.

Strapping on my blue armband, I meditated on my strategy. We would be separated into groups of twenty or so and put in storage houses scattered around the facility. As a blue, I had to get to the tallest building in the center but only during the ten-minute window. For the rest of the hour, I'd be playing cat and mouse with the reds.

The weight on my chest got heavier as my thoughts shifted to the demand Gray had given me this morning.

"What did he want anyways? What were these expectations I had to meet?" I wondered as I opened my locker and pulled out my vest and other gear. The vest had blinking blue lights attached to it like something you'd see in a laser tag game. Holding it up straight I noticed where all the targets had been placed.

My eyes narrowed in judgement. "Well they sure made that easy for the Reds, didn't they?" I muttered.

After pulling on the dark under shirt and combat pants, I noticed the vest was fitted perfectly in the back. I didn't even have to maneuver my wings in it to fit.

How nice of them.

I folded my uniform and put it back in my locker. I was strapping on my armband when the door opened.

I froze when I recognized the annoying tones that began to echo around the room. Dread was all I could feel. I wanted to hurry and leave. But their footsteps rounded the corner. Silence followed the abrupt cut in conversation.

"What are you doing here?" Trevor sneered.

Austin chuckled behind him, and I shrugged. Why they couldn't avoid me like everyone else?

"It's a shame, Ascella, I'm sure we could've been friends if you were normal."

"Good thing I'm not," I grumbled under my breath as I stood up to leave.

"Excuse me?"

I took the opportunity to get out and slam the door behind me. I was walking down the corridor when a hand caught my forearm. Austin appeared in front of me and grabbed my other arm. Catching on, I knew I was going back into the locker room.

I looked around in panic. No one was here. I twisted my arm to break the grip, but with no luck.

Well, crap.

Back inside, I was slammed against the cement wall.

"Listen up, chicken-wings, don't talk to me, I can mess you up good if I want," Trevor said while landing a kick to my knee.

I refused to give them the satisfaction of going down.

"What are you going to do when the government stops protecting your sorry case?"

Another kick.

"They should've just killed you along with your little freak family!"

A punch to the ribs.

The third kick caused my knees to buckle.

Trevor paused.

"Last thing, Ford, that son of a..."

I snapped. Next thing I knew, my knee had landed on Trevor's crotch. He howled and fell.

"Don't you dare say a word about my parents or Reece," I growled.

I would've said more but I was cut short by a punch to my jaw.

"Austin," I remembered.

Before I could get up, a foot pinned me to the ground.

Trevor loomed over me with a murderous glare and a snarl to keep him single forever.

I grabbed his ankle as the first kick struck.

The blows became painless as I closed my eyes. A few moments passed and black silence welcomed me into its arms of safety. When I opened my eyes, I was alone. My body throbbed and screamed in pain as I sat up. This was something Reece could never get involved with.

Checking my reflection in the mirror, I realized that my body would have some nice bruises in half an hour or so, but I could use the simulation as a cover up when Reece finally does see the marks.

I sighed and smoothed my hair before exiting and going to the big room where Reece would be.

"Will!" I heard Reece's voice call as I walked through the entryway.

I made myself smile when we made eye contact.

"Dude. What's wrong?"

I panicked.

"What are you talking about? I'm good."

Reece looked at me apathetically not buying my lie.

"Dude, we already went through this, don't keep things from me."

I had to make something up real quick.

"I'm just nervous," I blurted, and mentally facepalmed myself for how stupid I sounded.

"About the simulation? Come on man, you got nothing to worry about," Reece assured me patting my chest. I wanted to scream at the reignited pain but bit my tongue to keep it in.

"Will! Reece!" a feminine voice called from the mob of people.

I turned my head and saw Liz squeezing her way through to get to us.

"Hey Liz," Reece greeted.

I waved.

"You excited?" she asked.

"You're doing the simulation?" I asked.

The female laughed as if I'd quoted the meme of a lifetime, but suddenly stopped.

"No."

Reece joined her then added, "Bird brains, over here, is nervous."

I narrowed my eyes at the nickname.

"Don't be nervous Will, you'll pass it no problem," Liz comforted.

"That's exactly what I told him!" Reece exclaimed.

"Shut up," Liz snapped. "He hasn't done as many as you have, Mr. Only-Failed-Twice."

Reece's face changed dramatically, and I couldn't help but laugh.

The bickering between the two gave me a little entertainment which took my mind off of both the incident from the gear bay and the simulation.

Suddenly, the bell rang and everyone went silent.

"We gotta go," Liz said. "Simulation's starting in a few."

"Right behind you," Reece chimed in.

I followed the two and became lost in my own worries

over it.

"Earth to Will? Earth to Will?" Liz asked, jabbing my side with her elbow.

I jolted and fluttered my wings while barely holding back the tears from the gentle blow.

"What were ya thinkin' 'bout Will?" she asked.

"Nothing," I mumbled.

"Thinking pretty hard about nothing," she said as she got closer to my face.

Ugh, someone please kill me.

"Sure you weren't thinkin' bout something...maybe someone?"

Did she think I was interested in someone?

If I was being honest about myself, the idea of girls in general was maybe the scariest thing. I wasn't perfect, and what did they want? Mr. Perfect.

"So?" Liz asked again.

I groaned, knowing I wasn't getting out of this.

"Yeah I was thinking about the simulation," I paused. "And, uh, Reece, could I talk to you later?"

The reaction I received told me that the two didn't expect that response.

"Uh-uhm, yeah sure, of course."

I looked into the faces of my friends who pitied me, and I instantly regretted asking. Why didn't I keep my mouth shut? I didn't need to involve Reece in this.

I scorned myself for thinking of involving the one person I said couldn't be a part of it. Now, he was gonna hear it all tonight.

Immediately, I distanced myself and entered a room full of people.

Reece grabbed my shoulder.

"Hey Will-" suddenly his voice was drowned out with the siren initiating the ten-minute warning before the simulation started.

With an apologetic smile, I removed his hand and walked away.

I headed towards the loading bay where I saw soldiers getting onto trucks. I felt a sudden touch and nearly jumped out of my skin.

Whipping around I came face to face with Reece.

"Hey, are you ready?"

"Well, guess we'll find out."

Reece smiled, "Good, get a teammate. Solo doesn't work for everything, ya know."

I rolled my eyes.

"Where'd Liz go?"

"She was seeing someone off, I think? Honestly, I don't know."

"Wow!" I exaggerated. "Wasn't she with you literally one minute ago?"

The truck I was to get on rolled up.

"Kick some butt out there, Will."

I grinned, Reece was such a soccer mom.

Moving with the crowd, I wondered what obstacles General Gray had chosen to bless me with. The metal groaned beneath the forty or more combat boots as we were loaded onto the truck. Once we were piled in, a thud from the side of the truck released us from the dock. The vehicle lurched into drive, and I stood in darkness surrounded by people who stood so close to me, I reconsidered whether I was claustrophobic or not. Seven minutes had passed when the truck slowed down.

The doors were thrown open and our driver and an officer stood outside looking at us.

I followed the other men and women out and into the small storage house that we'd stopped beside.

A hand pressed into my chest stopping me from entering. I looked at the officer.

"General Gray ordered me to give you this," she said.

I took it, saying thanks, before opening it.

"Impress me." Was all it read.

Go kill yourself, Gray.

I looked at the people I'd been placed with. I didn't know anyone.

Oh no, looks like I'm going solo.

Suddenly, I felt a tap on my shoulder.

"Looking for someone?" the guy asked.

"What? No, sorry, I was just seeing who I was with."

"Observant."

I wasn't sure if he was just being odd or fake.

"Thanks?" I replied.

"Wanna team up? Or you with someone?"

"Sure," I said, forcing myself to look happy.

"Awesome, so we need a strategy since we gotta survive this thing for an hour."

Who the heck was this guy anyways?

He began drawing an invisible map on the wall.

"So this is our storage unit and these are the others," he began as he ran a finger to the invisible units. "They're about twenty-three yards apart. This is the safezone in the middle here, but we can't get there until the ten-minute window so I think we should stay below the radar in these areas.

Crossing my arms, I pondered as I visualized it.

Avoid the Reds or beat them without getting my targets

shot or my armband stolen, no biggy.

"We can still pass if we have one target and our armband left, so we just need to avoid head to head fights where we're outnumbered," I muttered.

"Bingo! My plan is that we play a type of hide and seek. Your wings," he said glancing at my back, "are essential if we get caught."

Wait, wait...Was he expecting me to be able to fly us both out of danger?

"So I suggest-"

The boy's voice was drowned out with the same siren from earlier. The simulation had started.

The door to the storage unit raised letting in the bright moonlight.

"We need to go," my comrade said.

Slipping out the door, we both sprinted beside each other trying to get away from the horde of blues.

The boy cast a glance over his shoulder before turning a sharp corner that I nearly missed.

We were alone as we went down the alley and slowed to a walk.

"Where...to?" I huffed.

"Warehouses...over there..." he replied, pointing to the roofs peeking over the smaller buildings.

The warehouses?

"What are we gonna do? Hop from warehouse to warehouse 'til time runs out?" I asked.

"You got it."

He ran off and I followed until we came to the large building.

"Did they unlock them for us?"

"No," he answered.

"Then how do you…" I trailed off as my comrade knelt and began picking the lock.

In a matter of seconds, it fell to the ground making me cringe from the loud sound.

Was this cheating?... It was just my luck to team up with a sketchy lock picker.

"Clear the area when I open the door."

It was freakin locked! You think anyone's gonna be in there?

But I did what he asked. After getting into position, I nodded at him and the door was swung open. After a quick sweep through, I announced it clear. There was a pause before he slipped in and closed the door behind him.

"We should be good for now," Lock Picker said as he flipped on a flashlight and walked deeper into the warehouse. "We'll stay here for about fifteen to twenty minutes then hop to the next one."

"And if we run into trouble?" I asked him.

"Fight, I guess?"

I wanted to facepalm myself.

Darn, I thought we'd sit down and sip tea.

"We need to keep watch," the boy continued. "You can fly, so I'll let you take care of it."

"Gee, thanks."

The Lock Picker smirked at me before I turned and took off. I landed at the small window that overlooked the door that we'd come in at. Hovering, I peeked out into the night outside. It was quiet and still, which was a relief but made me panic a little. I wondered if someone had seen us come in and were waiting to ambush us the moment we stepped outside. I shook the thoughts from my head and lowered myself to the ground before walking over to the Lock Picker to give a report. He leaned against the wall watching me as I walked up.

"You used to being on the run?" the boy suddenly asked.

I raised an eyebrow.

"Why do you ask?"

"S-sorry," the dark-haired male apologized with a blush. "Just rumors I heard."

We sat in an awkward silence before I decided there could be no harm in him knowing.

"I ran from the government."

Lock Picker looked up at me.

I sighed, knowing I was about to relive the past.

"I was normal, you know, I wasn't born with wings."

"You weren't?"

"Nope. They magically cursed my life when I got older," I said.

I turned and caught a glimpse of the name tag on Lock Picker's under suit.

"I was with my family when the government showed up to take us to who knows where." Jones was silent waiting for me to continue. "But my parents were shot and after being taken, I escaped for a few weeks. Eventually, I was brought back and here I am now."

The pain of my parents resurfaced but it was duller now.

"I'm sorry."

"Don't be."

"I don't get you," Jones began. "If I lost my parents I'm not sure what I'd do. Fifteen?"

"Fifteen," I confirmed.

Jones let out a soft whistle before saying, "Tough kid."

I wasn't sure how I felt about his comment, I certainly

didn't feel like a "kid" but at least he implied I was human.

"I-" I stopped short and listened to the sounds that came from outside. Jones fell silent too.

"Go," he whispered.

Slowly, I stood up and crept to the wall where the noise and voices were coming from. Pushing an ear to the wall, I attempted to make out the location and conversation but in vain. I stepped back and looked at my comrade who motioned me to fly up and check it out. I waved a hand across my neck telling him it wasn't possible. It'd be too loud. Then Jones began looking around the warehouse. I came over to him.

"What are you doing?"

"Looking for something tall enough so we can check out the commotion out there."

"How far is the next warehouse from here?"

"We shouldn't leave yet," Jones advised.

Looking to my right, I noticed what looked like the leg of a ladder behind a creepy door left ajar.

I walked to it and pulled out the ladder.

"How did I not see that?" Jones whispered harshly.

Bringing it over to the window, I climbed up and was barely able to see out the little peep hole.

My eyes widened.

Crap.

Quickly, I jumped off and moved to Jones.

"We need to go. Now." I hissed.

Jones' skepticism turned to horror as I explained the patrol of reds taking out a squad of blue right outside.

"Yeah, but why would they come into the warehouse?"

My mind immediately went to the lock lying on the ground outside. I knew we should have picked it up.

The door across the warehouse rattled suddenly. Jones cursed and scurried behind a pile of boxes with me behind him.

"Do you have a plan?" I whispered.

"Not a good one."

"But is it a plan?"

"It's a plan."

CHAPTER 9

IS MY BACK BLEEDING? I THINK I GOT STABBED

The door burst open and a group of five stalked in ready to fire. I analyzed them as they passed. The leader was a rather large guy, buff, broad shoulders and a short buzz cut, everything about him said 'trouble.' He was followed by two guys and two girls.

The guys looked average, but there was a macho girl that had an intense look, hopefully it was just a shell. I sized them up. If they weren't all together, then Jones and I might've had a chance in a one on one fight, but going at them in a group was like hitting the metaphorical "Fail Me" button.

I looked at Jones who gave me the signal to wait a little longer. The group looked as if they were about to settle in for the night.

We still had a chance. We'd hidden close by the door and if these Reds left the door open then we both could slip out undetected. Another figure came through the entry and looked right at my hiding spot. Could he see me? The guy looked away, and my fears were neutralized.

Glancing back at Jones, I squinted then realized he was counting down on his fingers. We were about to leave. I readied myself to use either stealth or speed. The countdown had ended, and I slid out from the shadows watching the group on the far end of the warehouse. The sounds of their low conversation echoed around the building. Jones followed me out silently as we passed through the door.

"Grab that lock," he whispered to me.

A questioning look came across my face as I wondered what he meant. Then I watched as he took the lock from me and grabbed the door handle.

This man was brilliant.

I watched Jones quickly close the door and lock it from the outside. Immediately, shouting and later banging on the metal could be heard.

"I cannot believe you," I whispered in shock.

"Oh well," he replied, before turning and beginning a swift sprint in the shadows lining the warehouse wall.

I spun on my heel and caught up to him.

"Let's skip the next warehouse," Jones informed me as we continued to keep good pace past what would have been the second hiding spot.

I noticed the shadows were getting shorter as the moon rose higher.

Suddenly, I heard a quiet outburst from Jones as he quickly dove back behind the shelter of the wall.

"What?" I asked, but Jones quickly put a finger to his lips with a wide-eyed expression. He indicated someone was behind the wall, so I switched places with him and had a look myself.

My eyes narrowed on a group I, for sure, did not want to see. I found Jones already backtracking to get further away from the group on the other side of the wall.

I followed him until we were a safe distance away.

"We can get past them," I said.

Jones looked at me puzzled, "How?"

"Can you scale this?" I asked, pointing to the wall behind me.

"It's possible. If you can anchor me to the roof, then

yes."

"Deal, and I'm telling you now that I've never flown another person before, but we're about to see if I can."

"Yeah, yeah...Wait what??"

I took the anchor from Jones that was clipped to his belt and took off to the roof. Who in the world had an anchor and cord for climbing just casually on them? Apparently, Jones did.

The only problem I didn't think about was hooking it to something. There was nothing up here. Well shoot. I decided that I could probably hoist him up myself since he wasn't that much bigger than me. Leaning over the edge I gave him the thumbs up then pushed my foot against the roof edge that came up a little providing a stronghold. I gripped the anchor and wrapped it around my waist just before I felt the weight of my comrade bear down on me pulling me toward the edge.

"Gah, what did you attach it to...oh," Jones trailed off as his head rose above the rooftop.

"Yeah there was nothing up here to attach it to," I explained as I unwrapped the cord from my waist and handed it back to him. My comrade looked at the gap that lay between the two tops of the warehouse.

"So you think you can fly us over- MOVE!"

Jones grabbed me and laid us flat against the roof just as a beam went above our heads.

I heard a curse a little bit away from us and turned to see a red from the party we'd worked so hard to avoid. My first thought was how did he find us then how the heck did that guy get up here?

"Ascella! Fly us!" Jones whispered harshly as he got up and began running to the gap. I Followed him at a sprint fueled with nerves and urgency. I grabbed Jones beneath his arms and made a rapid take off. I hadn't even realized I'd gotten us over until we'd passed the second warehouse completely and were coming up on the fourth, then I calmed down and felt the ache in my back, my wings, and my arms. My grip was beginning to loosen too. I lowered us in a glide that was too painful to be enjoyable and let Jones land in a run below me. With the added weight gone flying became significantly easier, but that didn't change how tired I was. I landed miserably and rolled to a stop. Jones was at my side in an instant.

"That was incredible," he breathed.

I groaned.

"Come on, Ascella. We gotta go."

I looked at his concerned expression and sighed.

"I won't be able to do that anymore, I haven't trained nearly enough to do that."

"It's alright! We can think of other ways to escape instead."

I nodded.

Jones took one of my arms and hoisted me up, supporting me over his shoulder. I looked back to see Reds trying to catch up to us.

"We gotta hurry."

I knew I had to push through it.

"How'd they find us?" I asked as we jogged across the roof.

"I have no idea, but they shouldn't have known we were on the roof, someone must have tipped them off."

The thought angered me as I knew it probably had to do something with Gray. He had all the access to the cameras and the administrators to do exactly that. "Impress him," that little-

"Will! Your left!!" Jones yelled.

Panicked, I jumped to the right feeling my ankle roll and my balance leave me.

To accurately put it, I was screwed.

Gravity took hold before I could recover. I toppled over the side of the roof and fell towards the concrete below.

I heard Jones yell my name after the impact, but everything was numb, limp, and blurry. My head spun as the realization of how much pain I was in crept in.

Forcing myself to sit up, I slowly regained focus and rubbed the back of my head.

Only then did I realize I was surrounded by Reds.

"Will!!" I heard Jones call.

His voice instantly made him another target and a show of lasers fired up at him. Using the opportunity, I got up and kneed one guy, took his gun, and took care of the ones that were closest to me. Building up courage, I got trigger happy and began taking out more until I'd shot down a good number.

Only then did it backfire and cause all of the guns to be trained on me. Someone from behind gripped my wrists as another kicked the gun from my hands. Quickly, I retaliated. Twisting my wrists free, I swung the guy over me and into the ground.

If there was one thing that Reece made sure I knew, it was hand-to-hand combat.

I turned to another and started with a hook to the jaw and ended with an elbow. I was like the Santa of bloody noses and pain right now and I don't think I've enjoyed giving out presents more.

I was the target of three in an instant. Soon my arms

were caught, and I could only struggle in my outnumbered condition.

"Jones! Help me!!" I yelled in dismay.

Through the mangle of limbs, I saw my comrade standing there with no intention of helping me. My trust in the guy was broken as he turned and made a quick getaway using me as a distraction.

Suddenly a voice behind me spoke up, "Guess he wasn't a good replacement for that Reece friend of yours."

The insult enraged me enough to give one last fighting kick, but I was wounded and shaken, there was nothing more I could do.

Why weren't they just shooting me and getting it over with? I wondered.

The hands behind me grabbed my shoulders and forced me to the ground, erupting a whole new set of pain. I saw someone stand in front of me. Looking up, I was reminded of what terror was.

"Look what the cat dragged in," Trevor menaced while dangling a coiled rope from his palm. "Boy, are we gonna have a little fun with you."

I winced. Surely, Jones was coming back.

"Did you really believe that we'd just shoot you and call it a day? Where's the fun in that?"

Wow, what a psychopath. Someone call the mental hospital and check this kid in.

Trevor laughed, "You've got a nice little price on your head and if we push ya around a little it'll be payday."

The group chuckled and snickered when he emphasized his air quotations.

Trevor knelt down to my eye level and whispered with a glint in his eyes, "Now just between you and I, I wanna thank you for being my free pass ticket, send my gratitude to the general."

I wanted nothing more than to rip his face off in the slowest and most excruciating way, then do the same to Gray. Jones must have set me up since the beginning.

"Really, it's been an honor, Ascella," he slurred sarcastically before turning to his comrades. "You three come with me, the rest of you go kill some Blues."

The group hooped and hollered, making me sick. Then I was picked up and dragged towards the nearest warehouse.

CHAPTER 10

GRAB YOUR STICKS! I'M A PIÑATA!

I wanted to puke after the fifth kick to my stomach. A hand grabbed the collar of my shirt making my eyes meet Trevor's.

He started talking, but his voice sounded distorted. My eyes couldn't focus.

"Look at me when I talk to you! You son of a…"

I slid my eyes back into contact with his and I was met with brown irises filled with hatred. My body was shutting down, everything was going numb, and a sense of unconsciousness nipped at my heels.

Trevor smirked and let go, letting me fall.

"You think you're so high and mighty because those mutations on your back make you so indispensable. But you were betrayed by your own comrade and by everyone else!"

Another hit to my wing spread pain all over my shoulders. A deafening silence followed until Trevor spoke again, "I'm done, I'm joining the rest of the group. You know what the general said, so make sure you break him."

My armband was ripped off. The other three approached me as Trevor left.

My armband…. if I'm gonna pass, I have to have it.

The biggest of the three crouched down and grabbed my jaw. He looked at my face in his hand.

"Looks like the others are gonna miss out on the fun."

The guy released me, "I bet you're wanting an explanation, so here it is short and sweet. If we break you, bingo, a free pass."

I wanted to defend myself, but my entire body hurt.

There was a redhead that came to my right and a brunette that came to my left lifting me up by my arms. I yelped. Black Hair came up to me with a wad of cloth in his hands.

Oh. Heck. No.

"Give me some help, fellas."

The grips on my arms tightened and my hair was grabbed, yanking my head back. My mouth parted and to my horror, the cloth was shoved in. My wrists were lifted against my will.

I squirmed trying to fight with anything and everything.

"Someone got a drug? The chicken's got rabies," said the redhead.

Surely they wouldn't have been able to bring drugs.

"Just knock him out or something."

Were they gonna beat me while I was unconscious?

Black Hair then slid behind me and I knew. I braced myself.

The metal hit my head and I wanted to scream from the enormous pain. I heard a curse then felt a second hit relieve me into darkness. It was only for a short moment. I came back to what I wanted to escape from so badly. I heard the voices and realized I could do nothing else but listen. I felt paralyzed. The voices I heard, jumbled as if submerged underwater. But the sounds gradually became clearer. I opened my eyes and saw the floor beneath my feet.

Was I standing?

My hands were tied up. I panicked as I realized I was suspended.

"Rise and shine, princess."

I looked up. Black Hair stood in front of me.

Where were the others?

"I have a question for you."

"Shut up," I snarled.

Black Hair snapped his fingers. Suddenly, cords that had been wrapped around the base of my wings began pulling in opposite directions. The pain was excruciating.

I grunted.

"I'll ask one more time-"

I spat at his feet.

I spat at him. It was what little I could do to save my pride.

Black Hair snapped his fingers again and the pain intensified. I thought I could handle it, but I couldn't. I screamed as my back was torn in two. The pain only got worse. I felt my tendons being slowly stretched and bones being close to being pulled out of socket. They pulled harder.

Black Hair walked away and came back with a metal pole in his hands.

"Ya'll go ahead and give him all ya'll got," he called.

No.

I was branded by the pain as it increased.

"Stop!" I screamed.

Black Hair only laughed as I failed to control the tears rushing down my face.

"STOP! PLEASE!"

My lungs hurt as the intensity of the pain could be heard in my voice. My vision began to blur. It hurt. It hurt so bad.

"Please...stop..."

My voice had been reduced to a whisper as darkness began closing in.

Black Hair stepped to my side.

"Night, princess."

He swung the pole and the impact to my ribs sent blood gushing into my mouth. I could no longer breathe, but I was saved from the suffering by the black of unconsciousness.

I jolted awake and found myself beaded with sweat. Immediately, the throbbing in my wings was magnified the more awake I became. I stared at the ground. The veins in my neck pulsed. My eyes were hurting and my whole body was in pain.

I looked around and found myself alone.

Oh no... was the simulation over?

I tried moving but I was still tied up. Looking down I examine the black and blue bruises that covered my torso. Even my amateur diagnosis could tell I'd broken something.

"Golly, if you hadn't been throwing a fit during your nap I would've pronounced you dead," said Black Hair.

"Just let me go."

"Oh you'd like that wouldn't you, but it's not on my to-do list."

He snapped his fingers. I was met with pain rawer than before. But something changed.

"What...happened...to...the...questions," I rasped.

Black Hair smirked at me, "We've passed that stage."

Go kill yourself.

I could no longer scream. My voice had been ruined but I smiled.

Black Hair got closer to me.

"Whatchu smiling about, Ascella?"

Chills ran down my spine.

"Thinking," I grunted.

Black Hair was looking at me viciously.

"Ya'll rip his flippin' wings off!"

The cords pulled harder, but I pulled back. I had no idea what my body was doing but it was better than hanging around and taking it.

"How's that, Ascella, a little more to your liking?"

I threw my head forward and head-butted him. He stumbled back, clutching his face. The cords slacked and the redhead and brown hair emerged. The redhead was holding a knife while brown hair looked like he was gonna pee himself.

Redhead charged.

Frick.

I swung to the side dodging his blade. This kid had an intent on killing me. I swung back around and zeroed in on the knife. I needed that.

It hurt worse than hellfire, but I used my wing and landed a blow to his stomach. He dropped the knife. My feet grabbed it and I grabbed the cords bending my body so my feet would reach my hands.

A punch landed on my back, and I dropped the key to my freedom. Brown hair picked it up and looked at me fearfully.

"What are you…"

That's an awfully stupid question.

I didn't answer, but I was tempted to say a piñata because I sure felt like one.

Brown Hair charged and I barely dodged in time. He grazed my side, and I was sure he clipped a few feathers.

I swung back around and realized this little party game would continue. I had to go up.

I gripped the rope and felt adrenaline rush through my veins. I climbed.

My arms felt like they were going to fall off, but it was better than getting stabbed to death. So who am I to complain?

They started whooping at me from below and calling my name.

"Come on down chicken wings, we won't bite."

That threat was lame.

My grip began shaking. I wasn't gonna be able to hold on much longer.

Suddenly, Brown Hair threw the knife at me.

I let go and felt the cords snap. My back hit the ground. I was free, but that last impact had been the final blow. I laid there, unmoving.

"Aw, is Willy all tuckered out?" one of them jeered.

I didn't answer. I couldn't. Something…. something was wrong. My body was on fire. My eyes flared up in pain and everything around me got louder. Suddenly, my chest cramped. My heart.

I clutched at my chest and felt tears stream down my face.

I heard their insults fade.

"If he dies, Gray'll kill us!" I heard one of them whisper. For just a whisper it seemed as if he'd yelled it.

I stood up and looked at them. I could hear all three of them breathing as if right into my ears and my vision was tinted red at the corners though it was abnormally clear. My senses had escalated several levels and so had my aggression.

Locking eyes with Black Hair, he slowly began backing up.

Kill them, my subconscious whispered.

I can't.

Sure you can.

Maybe… We'll see.

I stepped towards them. My body flew into a series of

motions. I kicked Brown Hair in the stomach and elbowed Black Hair in the face. Catching Redhead's punch I flipped behind him and kicked his back. Brown Hair was up and at me again. He landed a punch to my jaw, I blocked his kick. I threw his leg up and watched him fall back. A smile crept to my lips. I didn't know what possessed my body, but it was awesome.

"What the..?"

I turned to black hair who was eyeing me suspiciously.

"What?" Redhead asked.

"Look at him...his eyes..."

My eyes? What was wrong with them?

"Listen, we really had no intention of hurting you, we were just following-"

I uppercut Black Hair's stomach and watched him fall, curling into the fetal position.

"Shut up, I'm not buying that crap!"

Walking over, I picked up the metal pole that I'd been beaten with. I heard Brown Hair shout and I spun around, slamming the pole into his head. He collapsed unconscious. He'd be fine, but it wasn't like I cared anyways.

I knelt and ripped his armband off. That was one, two more to go.

"YOU SON OF A-" Black Hair began to shout.

I thrust my wing into Black Hair's torso and sent him rolling back. He sat up and glared at me. I ran and predicted his move. He punched and I blocked gripping his hand. I kicked him twice and threw him back. Black Hair fell then got up charging me. He caught my uppercut and the pole I'd swung down on him. He twisted the pole from my grip and threw it aside.

"You thought you could win?"

"You think I can't?"

Suddenly, a sharp pain exploded as a knife cut into my side. I'd forgotten about Redhead. I fell to the ground. I clutched at the wound trickling blood.

I grit my teeth and pushed myself away from them. They came closer.

My back met the wall.

"It's over, Ascella," Redhead said.

"No, it's not."

I threw the broken cord dangling around my wrist and made contact between Redhead's legs.

This is it. If I don't win now, I'm not going to.

Redhead howled and hit the ground. The pole was so close. I reached with my fingers and brushed the tip of it. My fingertips touched it again making it move. The metal rolled into reach, and I swung it at my two assailants. The impact on his skull made a ring. Redhead collapsed unconscious and brown hair stumbled back. He looked at his unconscious buddies, then to me. His face twisted in fury and terror.

"I'm gonna freaking kill you!"

He picked up the knife and charged. I pushed myself away, but he was faster. I blocked the first strike with the pole and pushed him off. I threw an uppercut to his jaw, but it didn't carry the strength behind it. Brown Hair grabbed my wrist and brought the knife down. I narrowly dodged it. The knife hit the cement.

Now!

I brought the pole around and hit the guy's rib cage. His eyes rolled back, and his body collapsed on mine. I pushed him off and took a moment to catch my breath. It was finished. Sitting up, I held my side. Examining it, I realized the knife hadn't gone too deep which was a relief, but it didn't relieve how bad the pain was.

I needed to get out of here. One of them could wake up at any moment. Using the wall for help I stood up and limped to black hair. Taking his armband, I searched his vest for anything useful. Nothing. I did the same with the other two and in addition to their armbands, I found a tablet-looking thing. I turned it on.

"Now what the actual…"

Red and blue dots crawled on the screen. It was a map of the entire area.

This has got to be cheating.

Suddenly, the message dropped down. It was from Trevor.

His name reignited my fury and the feeling from earlier. That adrenaline had saved me.

Maybe I should pay him a little visit.

I looked around and saw my vest laying on the ground along with my shirt in the corner. Going over to them I picked up the shirt and tied it around my waist in hopes of doing a DIY, Band-Aid edition. I pulled my vest on too and checked the pocket to see if my small pistol was in it. It was.

I typed in my name and the coordinate map zoomed in on what I could assume was Trevor due the pack of blue dots surrounding my green dot. With this, I could avoid trouble.

Suddenly, I paused. I felt good, but everything hurt.

It was another adrenaline rush.

Is this what Gray wanted?

Outside, I tried taking off and nearly broke down crying. It hurt so bad. But I tried again and began a light glide towards my armband's location. I settled behind a corner and scouted what I was dealing with. I saw a band of seven or eight. I wanted to instantly lurch at them and fight with sheer anger. But I would be beaten in seconds. I had to be smart. I looked at the ceiling of the warehouse and had an idea.

I limped to the other side and found a ladder to the roof.

Laying down I took out my pistol.

"Alright, adjust it to a long-range, and we'll see how far that'll get me."

I focused on the target and lined up my barrel with his vest. I engaged and it flashed white. I kept myself from chuckling as I shot him again as he searched frantically for the source. I smirked as his vest ran out of lives and I went on to the next one. Finally, the group took cover. I watched as some scattered and Trevor took off. I watched him run along the warehouses, a fist full of blue armbands. My eyes narrowed and I smiled. I aimed for him and shot his vest. I got down and followed the scared little punk till I saw him disappear behind a corner. I entered the alley behind him.

"A little cocky of you to go solo, don't you think?"

Trevor looked at me like he'd seen a ghost.

H-how...?

Walking over to him, I grabbed his collar and smashed his face into the cement wall.

"Ascella..." he grunted, peeling his bloody face off.

"You know why I'm here, don't you?" I snarled.

"...You're injured."

I glared. Pulling out the map from my vest pocket, I turned it on.

"This might show you."

Trevor reached for his gun, but I grabbed his wrist and bent it back.

"How did-"

I backhanded him.

"Just shut up," I snarled. "Every time you talk, you waste my time."

Trevor smirked at me. Why was he smirking?

Suddenly, his wrist was ripped out of mine as he rolled to the side and landed a blow to my stomach.

I doubled over clutching my side. The original pain was nothing compared to this.

"So you are injured. I see my friends did a decent job even though they didn't finish it."

"You're sick, you know that," I groaned.

His foot hit me in the head. My vision saw spots. I wasn't focusing and blood began trickling down my head.

My adrenaline was dying.

Another kick to my stomach and another as my body screamed that it couldn't take anymore.

I saw my vest flash, but never knew when I was being shot.

"This is why," Trevor snarled in between kicks. "Those who are on the bottom don't defy the top."

Unconsciousness threatened me.

Chills ran down my spine. It was coming. It was coming back. I felt the adrenaline take over my veins and was conscious of it.

I caught Trevor's next kick.

"What the??"

I shoved my knee into Trevor's groin then leaned against the wall in exhaustion. I pushed myself off and came over to Trevor.

"You know what, Ascella, I'm gonna-"

I sent an uppercut to his jaw making him fall back.

"What part of shut up did you not understand."

My anger resurfaced. I jabbed at his nose and heard a crack.

Trevor screamed as he grabbed his face.

I grabbed his bloodied collar and brought him up to my face.

"If you ever come near me again, I won't break just your nose."

He locked eyes with mine.

"Whatever."

I dropped him and stood up.

"Armband. Now," I demanded.

He grumbled as he handed the mass of blue armbands to me.

I snatched them from his hand and decided I'd get my revenge when I didn't feel like I was gonna bleed out at any second.

Suddenly, my vest flashed white. I'd been "killed" or so I thought. It was a second but then my lights came back on.

I'd been hit shot three times, how was that possible? Was this Gray's doing as well?

But my mind was quickly drawn away from the extra life I'd been blessed with.

Turning, I saw Trevor standing there leaning against the wall with his gun aimed at me.

Trevor took a step towards me, and I did the same.

I should've known better than to have turned my back on him.

"You look like you've seen a dead man."

"You'll be lucky to not be one after this," I growled.

Unfurling my wings, I grabbed him and let my malicious intent take over. Anger powered each wing beat as I took off into the night air dragging the writhing human behind me.

"Are you trying to kill me?! Is that what you want??"

Don't tempt me.

I rose higher into the sky. It was a struggle for me, and Trevor knew it. My body had taken too much. He grew silent as I hovered.

"Are you satisfied?" he asked me.

My grip loosened.

"What the- ASCELLA!! WHAT ARE YOU DOING!!!?!"

"If you're so superior," I slurred, "then save us both."

Trevor paled as I let go.

He screamed as gravity took control. I folded my wings and began my own free fall.

I put my hands behind my back and crossed my legs as I fell to further my point.

"You win! YOU WIN!!"

I ignored him, enjoying the show.

"ASCELLA!!!!!"

I saw the ground coming closer. I needed to catch him now if he was going to live. I nose-dived. He wasn't that far, but still, I hadn't thought through the landing. This was on impulse. I gripped his vest from behind and he screamed at me.

"I HATE YOU! I HATE YOU!" he repeated.

"Would you shut up! You're so annoying!" I yelled over the wind.

Spreading my wings, I strained under the weight. I tilted upward and pulled the extra body with me. It hit me harder than I imagined as I nearly killed us both. I leveled out and neared the cement and released him. I watched as he landed on his feet and rolled. I quickly landed and folded my wings. It'd be a while before I could do that again. The adrenaline was gone.

"Stay away from me!" Trevor gasped, standing up.

I ignored him.

"Don't bother me, and I won't bother you, understand?"

I didn't wait for a reply. I got away from him as soon as I could.

As I walked away, exhaustion flooded my system, but I still had to muster enough energy to win.

Using the coordinate map, I avoided contact with any Reds. Such a device had to be cheating, it was too much of an advantage. As I rounded a corner, a siren blared.

The safe zone was open.

I walked towards the main building since my wings were out of commission for the moment. Five minutes later, the siren sounded again.

As I got closer, I heard sounds of fighting and yelling on the other side of the warehouses.

Great, I have assured a fight around the entrance. I began to find strips of cloth and a loaded pistol that I went ahead and kept.

I came across a ladder leading up to the roof of a warehouse. For the first time in my life, heights scared me. But this was my best bet. Another siren sounded. I climbed to the top to find a large clock illuminating the top of the main building.

Two minutes left.

How was I supposed to get from here to there in less than two minutes! I stood there pondering what options I had. I should have stayed on the ground and fought my way through, but I had no strength. I could make it by air, but I didn't have the strength without adrenaline. Exhaustion was the only fuel I was running on. I'd been stabbed for crying out loud.

Another siren, one minute.

Taking one last look at the main building's doors, I outstretched my wings, backed up, and ran.

I leaped off. Approaching the doors at an alarming speed, I realized I was going too fast. My form fell. I spun out of control and collided with metal.

I breathed heavily and crawled into the fetal position. I'd made it.

"Are you okay??" I heard.

I heard another voice further away.

"What the heck?"

"He just crashed in here."

"Look at all the armbands."

"That's a lot of blood!"

"Somebody get a doctor!"

"He's not responding!"

"No," I croaked. "I'm fine."

I heard the last siren ring out in an octave higher than the rest. The simulation was over. Suddenly, an intercom echoed throughout the building.

"Congratulations, you've passed the simulation, for the next few minutes you will be sorted then briefed on your results. Please see the representatives posted at the North, South, and East corners."

The intercom shut off and the crowd that'd gathered around me disappeared.

I crawled over to the wall and leaned against it allowing myself to rest for a few moments.

"Are you sure you're okay?"

I looked up. It was the girl again.

"Yeah, I'm okay."

"You look like you've been through hell and back."

"Cause I have."

The girl looked me up and down again.

"I'm okay, I just need a second."

"Alright."

I watched her leave and appreciated the concern. Wish I'd have had her as a partner. The pain from everything was getting worse but I tried not to let it dictate the way my body acted.

I forced myself up and made my way to the closest corner. My steps grew heavier as I walked. Leaning against the wall, I clutched my side. My head began to spin.

I found myself standing in the lobby that served as the East corner. My nausea was getting worse. I leaned against the wall again to gain a little comfort as I joined the mass that packed around the door.

It seemed like an eternity had gone by until the official called my name.

"Will Ascella?"

"Present," I replied.

The woman, who held a clipboard to her chest, took a double look at me.

"Please follow me, do you need assistance?"

Now that was just downright embarrassing.

I forced myself up.

The woman led me down a hall and stopped at a room.

She knocked on the door before opening it and stepping inside, "I have him, sir."

I entered after her and found myself too tired to feel angry.

"Thank you," Gray said.

The woman left us alone.

"Sit down, Will. I want to chat with you."

I hoped it was a quick chat because I felt like I was gonna pass out. As I sat down, my entire body went numb. Gray began talking, but the ringing in my ears made it so I could focus on nothing but my discomfort. I swallowed. The last thing I saw was Gray reaching for me as I closed my eyes.

When I woke up, I was in the infirmary. An IV tree stood by my bed connected to my arm. I laid there quietly for a few minutes, as the previous events came back to me in pieces as I pushed myself up.

My fingers touched someone's arm. I saw Reece totally out on the side of my bed. It was good to see him. I looked out the window. It was early dawn.

Dang, I was out for a while.

Suddenly, a soft knock came from the door. I watched a nurse come in and begin filling out paperwork at the kitchenette. She turned and looked up.

"I'm so glad to see you awake, Mr. Ascella."

Mr. Ascella? That's fancy.

I didn't really know how to respond to her.

"Wait here, I'll be back with your medication."

I was on medication?

She left and I looked back at Reece who was still out like a light. My eyes saw blue and black bruises on my arms, and I honestly didn't want to see what the rest of me looked like.

The door opened again, and the nurse came back with a man in a white coat.

"Mr. Ascella," he greeted me warmly, "I'm glad to see

you up."

The doctor pulled up a stool, the opposite side of Reece, and began asking me questions.

"How are you feeling?"

"Good," I replied.

"That's good, any pain?"

"Errrrm, no, not really."

"Are you dizzy?"

"No."

As he asked me a hundred classic questions, I watched the man take the IV out of my arm and bandage it up.

"Could you look at me, Will?"

I had nurtured a hatred of doctors since Anna, but this guy treated me more like a person.

I watched the brown eyes study mine and noticed the features on his face. He had scruff and jet black hair that was slicked back.

"How have your eyes felt fine since the simulation?"

My memory drifted to the warehouse incident. I wondered if those three guys were here too.

"Um, good?" I answered cautiously.

"Wonderful!" the doctor affirmed as he clasped his hands together. Suddenly, Reece jolted up.

"What time is it?" he said.

I chuckled.

"Sleep good?"

Reece looked at me blankly for a moment.

"Will! You're alive!!"

"You make it sound like I was dead."

"You probably should be."

"Nah."

"I'll have the nurse administer your medication," the

doctor interrupted. "Do you need anything or have any questions before I go?"

I shook my head.

"Good, take care of him, Ford."

The doctor held out a hand for me to shake. "It was a pleasure to meet you, Mr. Ascella."

Wow, I hadn't been complimented like that in a long time. It felt nice.

The nurse came over to my bedside with a napkin and a glass of water.

"Please take these."

I took the cup and the two capsules that were in the napkin. As I swallowed the pills, the nurse went back over to the kitchenette.

"I need to go check on one more thing before we can release you. I'll be back."

The door closed and Reece glared at me.

"Dude, what the heck happened to you?"

"Yeah about that... I'll tell you tonight, I don't want other people to hear about it."

"I feel like you're gonna try to avoid it so once we're in our dorms, you're telling me."

"Sure."

Reece leaned forward and raised an eyebrow.

"Wanna come with me to the rec center after this?"

"No."

Reece looked at me dumbfounded. I couldn't help but laugh but immediately stopped. It hurt way too much to laugh.

"You know when I say I like you, it's just a reminder for myself," Reece jeered, clearly embarrassed.

There was a knock at the door.

"Come in!" I called. My smile was gone once General Gray strolled in. Reece stood at attention.

"Ascella, I'm glad to see you doing well."

I didn't reply.

"Ford, you're dismissed."

"Yes sir," Reece robotically responded.

He left and I was alone with this man once again. The General stood at the end of my bed.

"You may be at ease, Ascella, I'm here to discuss your results from the simulation."

I didn't realize how tense I was until I relaxed my shoulders and the rest of my body slouched. As I thought about my results, my anxiety returned. I'd let myself get kidnapped, shot, stabbed, and be stolen from. But this man had authorized it all.

"I'm proud of you."

What?

"As you know, I put a bounty on your head and gave the reds permission to push you to your limit if they managed to capture you."

Anger began to simmer in my chest.

"I had briefed them in hopes of triggering your fight or flight instincts."

This guy was a psycho. I rubbed my palms down my thighs and gripped my knees trying to keep myself from losing my cool.

"Will, look at me."

I looked into the man's dark eyes.

"Have you seen yourself, Ascella? Have you seen what I've pulled out of you?"

"No."

"You're angry. I can see it," the general said.

I hated it so much that if I didn't fear the consequences, I would've taken everything out on him.

"Your eyes show it."

Again with the eyes?

"I might as well tell you why I held this simulation. I was looking for an asset that your bloodline possesses. I needed to know if it'd been passed to you." He smiled. "You are a very valuable piece."

My bloodline?

I was getting some strong villain vibes, but what could I do about it?

General Gray placed a small, metal item on my bed.

"Look at this later, it may clear up what I'm talking about."

I nodded and glanced at the flash drive. The general stood up.

"Sir, will those who passed fight together on the frontlines?"

Gray looked at me.

"Ascella, who is Ford to you?"

Hold up. He definitely avoided the question.

I peered at him curiously.

"He is my comrade, sir, but I see him as my brother."

Gray nodded, "Let me ask you another question, you might find it hard to answer, but would you save Ford or yourself?"

"Reece, sir," I said quickly.

"Hmm, as I thought. Metaphorically, If the country was at war and depended on you and Ford were to leave, would you resign as well?"

I was confused.

"With all due respect sir, I don't believe I have the option to resign."

Gray's expression was like stone. Apparently, he found my comment neither funny nor amusing.

"I want an answer," he demanded.

Quickly, I gave one, "I would resign, sir."

"I see. I wish you a speedy recovery."

Gray took a few steps towards the door then paused, "You make a fine soldier, Ascella, a very fine one indeed."

Gray glanced over his shoulder at me, then he was gone.

I sat in silence and was a little shocked. That was weird.

CHAPTER 11

PHOTOSHOP'S EVOLVED OR I HAVE AN IDENTITY CRISIS

I walked out of the infirmary in my freshly cleaned uniform. Fresh air was always better than the smell of sick. I walked back to my dorm and touched the bandage wrapped around my side. It began throbbing again. I considered going back to get it checked on, but I'd had enough doctors for one day.

I trudged up the stairs. My door, 1224A, stood in front of me. Opening it, I went straight to my bed. My side of the room hadn't changed since I'd left yesterday. I sighed and changed my clothes into casual attire. I walked to the door and froze. I'd forgotten about my hair.

It wasn't that I cared, but I didn't want people screaming "His hair is as disorganized as my life!" or something along those lines. My reflection, unfortunately, redefined bad hair day. I took my comb and went to battle. I fixed my hair and turned to see Reece's laptop sitting on the edge of the bathtub.

"What- Why?" I gestured to the misplaced laptop sitting there. "Oh my god, Reece....."

I picked it up and took it over to his bunk.

The USB!

I searched my old clothes for the flash drive that Gray had given me. I slid it into the computer's jack and clicked on the application. The grid of photos popped up. I clicked on the first one.

Wow, what a perfectly normal picture.

I clicked on the next one and saw images of myself from various angles and locations. I was about to shut it off, but the next image caught my attention. A scowl formed over my brow. It was the warehouse. I clicked through the next few. I reached the part where I'd gotten free. My face was ugly as I rampaged.

What was Gray's deal about? Nothing is here.

I clicked again and fell silent. Someone had photoshopped my eyes red. I wanted to laugh.

Oooh the red-eyed bloodthirsty monster. Nicely done Gray, quite the character, no pun intended.

I flipped through the next and laughed.

They can't be serious.

I looked at the picture and noticed how awfully detailed it was.

Do we have a professional photographer on base?

I pulled the flash drive out.

This was just dumb. I put up the laptop.

They shoulda given me a metal arm or something. But what if it wasn't fake?

I wasn't playing that game. But it'd explain why everyone was flipping out about my eyes.

I started putting my coat on and walked out.

I had a valid point.

Undeniably, something weird had happened, so why not the fact that apparently, I'm now a superhuman with red eyes every time I have an adrenaline rush?

I entered the sliding doors of the Recreation Center. It was much hotter. I smelt sweat and cleaning chemicals. To my right, there was squeaking from shoes on the basketball courts and to my left, I saw doors leading to the weight room.

Where was Reece?

I avoided eye contact with the lady at the desk. There was no way I'd go up to her and ask. I could only imagine what that awkward conversation would be like.

Suddenly, an uproar caught my attention, it came from my right. I looked at the doors labeled game room.

That's probably my best bet.

When I entered the room, another uproar of laughter permeated the air.

"And you should have seen the look on his face," I heard Reece's voice as it got quiet again.

Oh no.

"Will had this look, it was the funniest thing I had ever seen! He was literally like…" Another roar of laughter.

That piece of trash!

I began pushing through the crowd getting closer to him.

"Then, you won't believe what he said after that! He said…." Reece trailed off when our eyes met.

Suddenly, he and I were the center of attention and I absolutely hated it. I raised an eyebrow and leaned against a column that was beside me.

"Continue. Tell me, I said?" I asked.

"Well, if it ain't the man of the hour!" John exclaimed, getting up from his seat and putting an arm around my shoulders.

The behavior of the group was acting odd. Reece walked over to the chair and stopped at the table holding a mini buffet of breakfast items. He poured out a cup of orange juice.

"Want some?" he asked me.

"No, and why won't you continue your little speech?"

"I know you do, and that was a good stopping point anyway."

No, it really wasn't.

Reece handed me a cup of orange juice. I sniffed it.

"What'd you do, poison it?"

Reece laughed, "No! I'm drinking the same stuff, dork!"

I took a small sip and my fear neutralized. It was actually orange juice. I noticed the crowd around us had begun breaking up, putting me more at ease.

"So what'd Gray talk to you about this morning?"

I took the donut Reece handed me.

"Yeah," I answered. "I passed out before he could talk to me at the simulation, so he just went over my results with me in the infirmary."

"Oh, that was it? Nothing exciting?" Reece asked.

I took a bite out of the donut.

The heck is this?!

I looked up and saw Reece smiling. He'd filled it with mustard.

I lunged at Reece. He tried to run but I grabbed him by the collar and smashed the donut into his face.

"How tasty is that?" I yelled.

John howled in laughter. The small group who'd seen the show began laughing too.

Reece wiped the yellow condiment off his face.

"I'll go get some paper towels before we get in trouble," John said.

Reece glared at me.

"I hate you," Reece spat.

I was all too happy to reply, "I hate you, too."

Reece and I walked out of the recreation center and towards our dorm.

"My face is probably going to break out tomorrow," he whined.

"I hope it does," I said.

I received a dirty look, but I didn't care.

"You're a butt."

"You started it."

We walked up the steps of our building and Reece opened the door.

"You took it to a whole 'nother level. My face still smells like mustard!" he spat as he walked in.

I shut the door behind me.

"You deserved it, for giving me a disgusting donut on purpose."

Reece stood in the doorway of the bathroom as he glared at me.

"If you'll excuse me, I am going to scrub my skin off to get rid of this smell!"

"Sounds good, Mustard Man."

He slammed the door.

"I am going to scrub my skin off to get rid of the smell," I mocked as I sat down.

"I can hear you!!" Reece yelled from the bathroom.

"Good!" I yelled back.

Suddenly, the bathroom door opened, and Reece popped his head out.

"Hey do you-"

A knock sounded at the door cutting him off. I walked over and opened it to see a girl in uniform.

"Are you Will Ascella?" she asked.

"Uh, yeah that's me."

"You're requested to be at the training center in ten minutes."

"Understood."

The girl saluted and walked away. I closed the door and sighed. It was like I couldn't enjoy just a moment's peace around here.

"Who was that?" Reece called from the bathroom.

"A chick who said-"

Reece popped his head out, "Was she hot?"

"I mean, sure? Do you even care what I have to say?"

"Oh yeah, continue."

I cleared my throat annoyed at the rude interuption, "Apparently, I'm wanted at the training center in ten so that's where I'm going to be headed now.

"What, why? What'd you do now?"

I shrugged, "Probably made another guy smell like mustard."

"Okay, stop."

I laughed and turned toward the door.

"I'm going now."

"I'll come with you."

"Mmkay."

I was already out the door and halfway across the lot when I heard Reece yell at me from the barracks.

"Really, Ascella?!"

I chuckled and continued on my way.

As I came towards the training center, something was off. I walked in and heard my name immediately. The secretary at the desk was looking at me.

"You've been requested in facility B," she said, sweetly.

I nodded and made my way through a pair of double doors. When I entered, my eyes landed on one face. Trevor.

Maybe he was back for round two. If he was, I might actually kill him this time. He made eye contact with me and began walking over.

Uh oh.

I felt my body tense as he got closer.

"Ascella," he nodded and then paused before walking past, "I don't know why, but Gray has been asking for your whereabouts."

I raised an eyebrow.

So he was helping me now? That's not at all suspicious.

"Thanks," I muttered.

Trevor walked on while I took in my surroundings. There were a couple of guys bashing it out on each other. But no Gray and no obvious reason for me to be here.

I moved closer to the brawl of the two. They were so methodical, moving so quickly and precisely.

I took notes of the patterns. A right hook, a left, then block, then a shift in weight.

"Ascella," a voice said behind me.

I jumped out of my skin.

It was Gray.

"You seem rather engrossed," he said, nodding at the two I'd been watching.

"Yes, sir," I answered.

"Intriguing," he commented quietly. "I know it is out of the ordinary, but I thought you and I should settle for a little conversing, no?"

That was maybe the weirdest way to say "Let's talk."

Gray turned and led me through some double doors, past the target range.

"In here, please," he said, holding open the door.

I entered the small conference room.

Gray took a seat at the head of the table, and I debated whether to sit next to him or at the other head of the table.

Least with that, I'd be the preferred distance away from him.

"Sit down, Will."

I sat at his right feeling like I was about to be given a secret mission or get my butt chewed out.

The general sighed before speaking, "Do you know who you are, Will?"

I'm sorry? Since when was I having an identity crisis?

I scrunched my eyebrows clearly confused.

"What I mean is, do you know your purpose?"

I thought for a moment.

Aside from being a scientific marvel, I had no idea what he was talking about.

I took in Gray's body language. He was flipping a gold coin between his index and thumb. The symbols on it were three triangles forming a larger triangle.

Where had I seen that before?

Suddenly, his hand grasped the coin. I looked up and saw Gray peering at me. Now I was concerned on a totally different level.

Gray leaned forward expectantly.

What'd he ask me?... My purpose!

"No, sir?"

Gray sat back in his chair.

"Well, you're very important. In fact, I would call you the catalyst for the future."

I looked at the general.

Was this a joke? Why was he being nice to me now? And important? The only thing that made me important was the fact that I could flap myself from point A to point B.

"I'm not sure I understand."

"I don't expect you to, but just know, I'll need you very

soon."

Gray pushed himself from the table and got up. I followed his example and stood up as well.

"Ascella, I have never told a soldier this, but I need you."

At that moment, I was so confused, I didn't respond.

What just happened?

I followed the general out the door.

Was it really necessary for me to have been called just for this?

So many questions filled my head that I felt it was displaying a system error notification.

Gray stopped before the double doors that led back into the sparring room.

"I have other matters to attend to. Excuse me."

I nodded and saluted out of habit. The general saluted back, then walked in the opposite direction.

I watched Gray's back narrowing my eyes in suspicion. Something about that felt weird, maybe even ominous.

Turning, I walked back into the sparring room. Only this time I saw Reece.

He turned as soon as the door shut behind me. He bounded over to me all smiley.

"Why'd you get called in here?"

"Eh, nothing big, I wouldn't worry about it."

Reece studied my face.

"I think you need a daily dose of hand to hand, come on."

"I'm supposed to be healing."

"I won't hit you that hard, it's fine."

I rolled my eyes and called after him.

"Why don't you teach me something new?"

Gray wasn't gone from my mind, but at least this was a good distraction. I didn't like the coin in his hands and Gray's "You're important" speech. Reece came over to me and lightly punched me, "Bro, you have to focus first if I'm gonna teach you something."

My eyes widened. Gray might target Reece. If he did, I'd kill him.

CHAPTER 12

DON'T EAT BURRITOS AROUND HALLOWEEN

The question haunted me again, "Do you know your purpose?"

The only lead I had was that he considered me a valuable piece, but that really didn't explain much. What puzzle was I an important piece in?

I heard Reece sit up on his bed.

"You good dude? You've been acting weird since the training center today."

"I'm good, just tired," I lied.

"Okay...but you know, you can always talk to me, okay?"

"Alright, I will."

"But hey, look at this!"

I rolled over and watched Reece hold up his hand like he'd just been engaged.

"Nice, when's the wedding?" I asked.

"My mom gave it to me, dork!"

I glanced at the ring again before turning my attention back to Reece.

"That's pretty neat, dude."

I thought for a moment about Reece's mom then felt the pain in my chest. I missed my family. Unconsciously, I reached for my dad's feather hanging around my neck.

Reece noticed.

"What was your family like?" he asked.

I paused.

"They were good people. Mom and Dad didn't deserve

what they did to them. They were really kind and always gave stuff to others. My mom used to tutor kids and my dad was always really good at technical things. He built me a robot for my eighth birthday and a bunch of other things. I felt that they maybe even knew. We spent so much time together doing things together until they died... I don't know." I took a shaky breath. "I wish they could've been here a little longer."

Reece was deathly quiet.

"Dad was always super smart and made my mom laugh a lot...uhm..."

Remember.

I recalled the time before my life had changed, back to Christmas and elementary school. Suddenly, I remembered an embarrassing story about myself.

"There was this one time," I began, "I'd won a soccer tournament and all the team and parents went to this Mexican restaurant across the street called Taco Chaco."

"Taco Chaco?"

"Yeah, I know. But it was around October and they had all these Halloween decorations up."

"Continue."

"As I ate my burrito, I saw this painting of a zombie with its organs hanging out. And you know, six-year-old me had a sensitive stomach."

"Yeah? And?"

"And I threw up."

"Wait, wait..." Reece stopped me. "A zombie picture was what made you throw up?"

I smiled shyly.

"Was it super gory?"

I looked down.

125

It was a cartoon zombie, but-"

"And how old were you???"

"I was like six, man!"

Reece laughed, "You were one sheltered little kid! Clearly, you needed some hardening up."

"What! No! My dad was ruthless! Whenever the Monopoly board came out, he took advantage of me! A seven-year-old kid! I was scarred for life after that!"

"You should play me!"

"No, absolutely not! I haven't played since!"

"Oh come on, surely it wasn't that bad."

Reece gave me a look before changing his expression.

"What about your mom?"

I looked down. The memories of her embrace after school and her singing in the kitchen came flooding back. I'd give anything to lose one more game to Dad and refuse one more kiss from Mom. I swallowed hard and felt the tears swell in the corners of my eyes. There was the time when I'd entered middle school and my mom had become increasingly affectionate. I missed her.

The tears began to swell up in my eyes again. Immediately, I tried to blink them away. I couldn't break in front of Reece. I swallowed hard. Forcing myself to smile, while looking at the floor.

"My parents were amazing. Sure, there were times I didn't like them, but every kid goes through that."

I looked at Reece who nodded at me, "I could say the same thing about mine."

"But my mom..." I sighed and chuckled. "I loved my mom. She was really healthy, you know, all about organic foods and stuff."

"She was?"

"Yeah, so I kept a stash of candy in my room and rationed it out."

"Bro, no way."

"Yeah, and it was awful because she had the nose of a bloodhound and I didn't have a brother or sister to blame wrappers on."

Reece laughed, "I'm guessing you got some stories then?"

I groaned, "Too many…"

I thought for a second.

"There was this one time I hid a cake from my mom and didn't get busted."

"Wait, like a whole cake?"

"Yeah..?"

"Golly! You monster! Where did you get a whole cake!?"

"Not important," I chuckled and rubbed the back of my neck, "but you know how I'm addicted to lemon?"

"I did not know that, but now I do."

"Anyways, I had this lemon cake, and oh man, literally the best thing ever made. So by the time I'd had it for a day, there was a little more than half of it leftover so-"

"You ate half of the cake!"

"I said less than half! And it's not like I had a personal fridge!"

"Will!"

"Let me finish!"

Reece began silently laughing.

"So while I was eating it in my room, I heard my mom coming up the stairs."

"Oh shoot."

"So I put it down but didn't have time to hide it. And

Mom walked in but here's the thing, she walked right past it. Didn't see it or anything."

"Where'd you put it?"

"Beside my desk!"

"Your desk?!"

"That's what made it so funny! I don't know how she didn't see it or smell it. And let me tell you, I felt as if I'd just escaped death itself!"

Reece and I roared with laughter. I rolled back onto my bed clutching my stomach.

Those were some of the best times of my life.

"I still can't believe you ate a whole cake!"

"Half!" I clarified, but after a moment I added, "but eventually whole."

I sighed wishing my life could have stayed that way.

My eyes began to burn as I fought back tears once more, but this time I couldn't stop them.

"I miss them."

My tears streamed down my cheeks, and I hid my face from Reece's gaze. I didn't need a mirror to know I looked broken. Going off of feeling alone, I felt broken.

"Sorry..." I muttered, as I wiped my face and forced a smile.

"Nah, man, you're good."

Reece patted my shoulder and sighed as he stepped back to his bed, "I'll let you sleep okay."

I nodded and pulled the covers back and settled onto my stomach relaxing my wings.

"Night, Will."

"Night," I muttered.

My breathing slowed and I closed my eyes. All I needed was sleep.

In my dream, I was lying on the ground under a cluster of trees. A mound of leaves and broken branches were around me. I'd been here before. I waited for the shouts of my hunters, but they never came. My surroundings turned to black, and I wondered if I was awake. I wasn't.

My dark environment changed into the cell I'd been kept in. Dr. Anna was speaking to me from the other side of the glass, but I couldn't hear her. I didn't move and kept the same position lying on the concrete floor.

Again, darkness came and the next scene appeared.

A door opened and a uniformed man drug me out from the vehicle that had abducted me. Gunshots rang out and when I managed to turn my head I saw my front door. It was a sight I thought I would never see again. My atmosphere changed into my living room.

Footsteps were heard coming down the stairs to answer the persistent knocking.

'Don't answer it!' I wanted to yell. But the figure I expected to see wasn't my dad, but my best friend. A panic came over me. Reece had opened the door and disappeared into the warm light. Immediately, I ran for the door and stumbled through it.

My feet fell on ash. I turned around. Everything from before was gone. Ash was the only thing I saw. The hair on the back of my neck rose. Something was coming. It was a wall of smoke rushing towards me. I wanted to wake up, I needed to wake up. But I just ran.

The ash was quicksand pulling me down. I stumbled over the top of an ash pile. The smoke gained on me as I continued through the never-ending landscape. Tumbling down the ash pile, I landed in a valley of bones.

A skeletal hand shot up from the ash and gripped my

foot. More hands came as I tried kicking them off.

I wanted to shout for help, but there was nothing I could do. In a moment the smoke wall hit me.

I sat up in a panic, kicking away the covers that had entangled me. It was still dark. I glanced at my alarm and decided against going back to sleep.

Looking over, a sigh of relief escaped from me.

Reece was there. I got up and checked on him.

Everything was okay, my head assured.

Pulling out my drawer, I did my best to stay quiet as I pulled out shorts and a tank top. I changed clothes and slipped on my shoes when I heard a mumble from the sleeping form across from me. I froze, becoming deathly silent until his soft snores came back. Then I slipped out into the morning air.

I reached the bottom of the stairs and walked along the sidewalk. Kicking to a jog, I followed the path weaving in and around the facilities. The simplicity of the morning was a nice change. No nightmares, no fights, no Gray.

The quietness of the morning made me relax.

I had completed two miles when I rounded the corner and slowed. There was a group of uniformed men working on the base of a building. An odd air developed as I walked by them. I glanced back and made eye contact for a brief moment. The man quickly looked down.

Were they even fixing something? They had materials around them, but I didn't see any problems.

I shrugged and pushed them out of my mind.

What would I know anyway?

When I reached four miles, I turned back and retraced my path. As I came back, the men were gone and the building looked the same.

I slowed to a walk when the stairs to my dorm came into view. The sky had brightened into a stormy gray.

It must be about to rain. When Reece wakes up I'll ask him about the workers and see if he knows anything.

I quietly opened the door and stepped inside, expecting to hear snores, but all I heard was silence. I walked further into the room and stopped when I saw the bed vacant. Reece was gone.

CHAPTER 13

I HATE THE ACT

I finished off my last target angrily.

"Who peed in your Cheerios?" the guy muttered beside me.

I ignored him and walked off to turn in the gun to the clerk.

It was four in the afternoon and Reece was still nowhere to be found. I was seething. My deduction led me to believe that Gray had something to do with it.

If only I hadn't been so stupid, saying I was more loyal to Reece than him. For all, I knew Reece could've been kidnapped and dumped in the middle of nowhere so that they could completely erase the lone obstacle to getting my full allegiance.

"Calm down," I advised myself. There was no way they could've done that. There was Reece's family, and the news and media that would get in the way of the government blatantly murdering one of their own. But I couldn't shake the feeling that something bad had happened to him.

I shoved the rifle back into its slot as the clerk came over to check it in his log.

"You killed it out there, Ascella!" he said.

"Thanks," I grumbled.

"I've never seen you take targets out that quick."

"Thanks."

"I'm serious, you have skills!"

I wanted to bang my head against the wall. This idiot couldn't tell the difference between murderous intent and skill.

I was imagining shooting Gray's face, was what I wanted to say but decided not to.

"Thanks," I replied again.

"Got any classes after this?"

Oh my gosh, please shut up.

"No sir," I replied.

"Well, enjoy your afternoon then and congratulations on passing the simulation!"

I forced a smile and gave a small salute. I walked outside with anger pumping through my blood.

If I saw Gray, I don't think I'd be able to keep myself from slitting his throat.

I found myself heading towards the recreational center. I passed the sliding doors and entered the lounge when a familiar face was getting coffee.

"John!" I called.

"Will? Hey, what's up?"

I sighed before answering.

"Reece has been missing since the morning. I can't find him anywhere and I think General Gray has something to do with it."

John had an expressionless look on his face before bursting into a fit of laughter.

"John, this is serious!"

"I know which is why it's funny."

"Do you know something I don't?" I asked, annoyed with him.

"Yeah, he's at the hospital."

"What!?"

"Whoa, chill out! I should've worded that better. His sister went into an experimental surgery this morning."

It was finally official. I wanted to rip my hair out.

You couldn't have told me sooner?? And sister?? I've never heard of her.

"Would've saved me a lot of trouble if he'd simply have let me know."

"Uh, you don't have a phone, and Reece said you were gone when he had to leave."

He had a point.

"Anyways, Reece has a sister?" I asked.

"Yeah, Payton?"

The name rang a bell. A very faint bell, but still a bell.

Maybe Reece did mention her...oops.

"She's been dealing with an odd form of cancer, and it's been a struggle for her."

"Oh, how old is she?"

"Oh uh, maybe about fourteen or fifteen."

She was close to my age, that had to be tough.

John took a sip of his coffee and looked at me.

"You can hang with me for the day if you've got nothing else to do."

I nodded, "Do you know when Reece will get back?"

John shook his head, "No clue. I haven't heard from him since this morning. But I need to head back to my office."

He turned and I followed him out of the rec. building and into the engineering one. When we got to his office he opened the door and I was shocked by how much technology covered the walls. He could've been the son of Bill Gates or even a rocket scientist.

"Welcome to my humble abode," he said with a mock bow.

"More like nerd land," I corrected. "What do you do with this much tech?"

"I'm an engineer, what did you expect?"

"Right."

I settled down into a chair while John picked up and began working on some sort of device. He poked and prodded at the wires and began taking them out. Suddenly, a knock sounded at the door.

"Come in," John called.

In walked the man I had intended to kill this morning. John immediately stood at attention, and I followed.

"Morning John, mind if I borrow Ascella?"

"No sir."

"Excellent, come with me," he said, turning to me.

I stood up and followed the General out into the hall. He closed the door to John's lair and led me outside to a hanger that I'd never been in before. Once inside, the heavy air that hit me was tainted with the scent of iron. It was unpleasant.

"Permission to speak freely," I asked.

"Granted."

"What is going on?"

"Well, I was looking at your course results and figured I'd amp things up a notch."

How thoughtful, thank you for your kindness.

"And why are they here?"

Gray followed my gaze to the scientists in white coats sitting behind a glass window.

"Oh never mind them, let's get started."

Excuse me??

Gray walked over to a box on the wall, opened it, and began tapping away at some sort of screen.

I was left standing very concerned.

Oh never mind them, I mocked Gray in my head.

135

"Ascella," a hand landed on my shoulder and I jumped. I whirled around to come face to face with one of the scientists.

"Would you put this in for me?" he asked.

I looked down and took the earpiece from his hand. Reluctantly, I put it on after making sure it wouldn't fry my brain or some nonsense.

"Give us a thumbs up, Ascella," I heard the transmission.

I did as I was asked and heard the voice come again.

"Alright, we'll be starting in three... two... one."

Starting what???

I stood there confused as I saw the room dim a little and a hologram form.

Luckily, I knew about holograms. They'd been merged with A.I. characteristics and semi- tangible properties over the past ten years. But the one in front of me was different. It was holding a gun.

It shot a bullet at me that shattered into a miniature fireworks show when it hit my arm. It was completely painless as if it hadn't been there at all.

This had to be a joke.

"Stop," the voice in my ear said.

The hologram froze and the lights came back on as a white coat came from the window room in the wall. He had wires or whatever hanging from his hand.

"Would you take off your shirt, please?"

How about no.

I was beyond skeptical, but what could I do about it, at least he said please.

The scientist dude hooked the wires to my chest and checked over his work.

"Alright, leave your shirt off please, it'll interfere with the sensory pads."

After he disappeared behind the door, the lights went dark again and the same hologram reappeared.

Another bullet was fired at me, and I could feel it this time. I gripped my side where it'd landed.

"What the heck are these things?!" I grunted

Not as bad as an actual bullet, but the pain was still pain. Two more holograms formed, one duel wielding a gun and a knife.

I grabbed the figure by the neck and pulled him forward as I prepared for the sharp turn. It wasn't the realistic reaction that spooked me, it was the fact that the hologram felt like an actual person. The figure fell to the ground and shattered, leaving me with the remaining two. I dodged the glowing bullet aimed for my chest and rolled under the barrage flying at me.

Frick! Frick! Frick!

I boosted myself with my wings to stick the landing and used them to create distance between me and the one holding the knife. I jumped above the first shot and the second, the stupid thing was shooting at my feet.

Overall, I had a shoulder and rib that stung. There was an opening, and I took it. I grabbed the hologram's wrist. I twisted it back to let the gun fall away. I'd pinned him when I felt a sharp stab in my back below my wings. I yelled and fell to the ground. Both figures stood still then shattered. The whirring cut off. The hanger's lights brightened suddenly. The sound of a door opening and closing echoed. It wasn't soon after that, feet began shuffling towards me. I looked up and realized my hands were shaking.

What are these pads?

"Get those sensory things off of him! You're sure there are no side effects of this? I need him to be at full capacity!" Gray shouted at, presumably, one of the scientists.

I felt someone's hands taking off the pads that were on my chest. When they did, the stinging from the bullets and knife began to subside.

One of the scientists helped me stand up.

I saw Gray and another scientist in a heated discussion about some sort of primary stage of the program. An acceptable answer seemed to have been reached because the conversation ended and the general made his way over to me.

"How are you, Ascella?" he asked.

"Just swell," I groaned.

"Good, how do you feel about written tests?"

The adjective written made dread spread throughout my body, but the noun test made me want to go kill myself.

"Do I have a choice?"

Gray laughed a little, "No."

I groaned as I was soon led into the window room that turned out to be a lot bigger than expected. My eyes fell immediately to the desk sitting in the corner with a scientific calculator on it.

Oh, come on! I just got stabbed and you want me to take something that involves a calculator?

As I sat down, a scientist handed me a packet. I looked through it suspicious of its blank cover. The first six pages were various math concepts, next was English, reading interpretation, and physics.

I looked at the man disgusted.

"This is an ACT."

I looked at the blank cover again wishing I could see

what form number it was. I'd taken plenty of practice and researched which form numbers were the easiest versions.

"It is part of an ACT," Gray said, handing me a pencil.

"I've already taken it."

"Not this one."

I looked at him for an explanation.

"It is a hybrid of the SAT, ACT, ASVAB."

If I could've seen myself at that moment I probably would've had a look mixed between hatred and horror.

Why not make a hybrid test for a hybrid human? Real funny.

"Please open to the first section, Ascella," a scientist said.

I did as I was told and looked at the first problem. Immediately, I wanted to cry.

It was a blank unit circle from trigonometry.

"Your time starts...now!

I laid on my bed that night completely exhausted. Stupid math, English, chemistry, all of it! At least, it was over. My hate for the ACT had been resurrected after that stupid test.

Suddenly, the door opened.

I sat up.

"Reece?"

My friend stumbled over to me and pulled me into a tight hug without a word.

"H-hey... what's wrong?" I asked, hugging my trembling friend.

"It worked," I heard him whisper, "My sister's cancer-free."

CHAPTER 14

CALM STREAM TO TSUNAMI

He sobbed as I tried to comfort him.

"I'm sorry," Reece mumbled.

He pulled away and wiped his tears.

"You're good, man," I said

My friend looked at the floor and grinned. I couldn't help but smile, I could feel the joy emitting from him.

"I can't believe the cancer's gone."

"That's awesome! When's Payton going home?"

"Tomorrow."

My cheeks began to hurt by how hard I was grinning. I pulled my best friend into another hug.

"I'm so happy for you... why didn't you tell me about the surgery beforehand though?"

Reece pulled away and avoided eye contact.

"You'd been through so much... I didn't want to burden you with my problems on top of that."

I sighed, "Next time tell me, you've been a friend to me, let me be a friend to you, too."

Reece's countenance fell, "you're right, I'm sorry."

I grabbed his shoulders.

"You don't need to apologize, I already forgave you."

"Jeez, when did you become the bigger person?"

I laughed at him as he headed to the bathroom.

"Will the lights bother you?" he called.

"Since when did light ever keep me from sleeping?"

"I dunno, I just thought I'd ask."

"Goodnight, Reece!" I called.

"Night!"

Once my head hit the pillow, I fell asleep immediately. It felt as if I'd slept for a few seconds when I woke up. I'd dreamt that dream again. The ash land, bones, and pursuing dark clouds were only becoming more disturbing.

I looked across the room at Reece who was asleep. If only I could sleep as soundly as him and not wake up before the crack of dawn.

Sighing, I swung my legs over the bedside and got ready for another morning run. I heard a groan, and I looked to see Reece squinting at me.

"Why the heck are you up?" he whispered.

"Couldn't sleep, so I'm going on a run."

Reece looked at me as if I told him I was going to frolic with unicorns in a field of rainbows.

"It's four in the morning," he said.

"Yeah?"

"What are you? An insomniac?"

"At this point, it wouldn't surprise me."

There was a pause then Reece rolled over, grumbling, "Weirdo."

By the time I'd finished getting dressed, Reece's snores had started back up.

I walked outside into the dark morning and the humidity hit me like a truck. It was darker than usual, and the air was heavy. Rain.

I decided that a quick run would be best since I hated getting my wings wet. Water just made them so heavy.

As I made my way down the stairs, I looked out. The base was quiet, but in an hour or two it'd be back to its busy self.

My footsteps were rhythmic along the path. I didn't see any of the men working on the buildings this morning which I found weird. I saw them yesterday morning and evening, each time working on a different building.

Maybe they've fixed everything?

My thoughts moved past it. Why should I even care about whether or not someone is updating a building.

When I finished running, the rain began to drizzle. I walked back to my room and found Reece in the bathroom. He peeked out from behind the wall when I closed the door.

"How wa yo wun?" he asked with the toothbrush in his mouth.

"Good, looks like it'll rain today. I don't know how heavy though."

"Wain's nice."

He beat his toothbrush and began getting dressed as I changed out of my sweaty clothes, putting on clean ones. Reveille began playing as we walked out the door and down the steps. The old trumpet tune was one of the last few traditional things they kept around after the major revolution of the military's workings.

"I know this is random, but have you ever flown in the rain?"

"Eh, not really, since that's kinda dangerous. Water makes it hard for me to stay airborne. Why do you ask?"

"No reason, I was just wondering since I've never seen birds fly in the rain."

"You're relating me to a bird?"

"Will, I don't know if you looked in the mirror this morning, but you have wings."

"What? Really???"

Reece rolled his eyes.

"Shame on me for comparing someone who has wings to something that has wings too."

"I know! The absolute audacity!"

Reece and I looked at each other straightly for a moment before bursting into laughter.

We entered the mess hall and merged into the line for breakfast. I grabbed my favorite combo of pancakes, eggs, and bacon, then followed Reece to the table where John and Liz sat.

"Hey, Reece, Will."

"John, how ya been man?"

"Good, how's the sis?"

Reece grinned, "She's coming home today!"

"That's wonderful!" Liz exclaimed. "I'm so happy about that!"

My ears heard nothing more of the conversation that continued without me. My gut told me something was off. I looked around at the tables full of other soldiers. I could feel someone's eyes on me. Nobody gave any weird signals around me though which was confusing. I turned back around. Was I imagining it?

"Will," I heard.

"Huh?"

I looked at Liz who peered at me concerned.

"I asked how your visit with General Gray went yesterday."

"Oh, uh, yeah, I guinea pig for some holographic thing and took a test."

"A test?"

I nodded.

"Wait, what about Gray?" Reece spoke up.

"While you were absent, Will was chilling with me, when the General came and borrowed your bud for the rest of the evening," John said.

"And he made you take a test?" Liz questioned.

I took another bite of my pancakes, that I'd drowned with syrup.

"Yeah, it was like a hybrid ACT or something. Real ridiculous in my opinion."

"How'd you do?" Liz asked.

"That was it?" John added.

I looked around us again. My instincts were going nuts, but I didn't see the danger.

"I got a 34," I mumbled.

The three looked at me.

"Aren't you like fourteen?" Reece asked.

"Fifteen, going on sixteen," I hissed.

John was the only one who didn't look as shocked.

"Figures," he said. "I made a thirty-six as a sophomore."

"Shut up, John, nobody cares," Liz spat.

John shrugged but didn't argue.

Liz was about to reply when she froze. She stared straight through me. I followed her gaze and paled. Now I understood, my gut was right. There was a soldier sitting in his chair with a clean bullet hole through his head

The blond slumped with his face landing on his plate. He'd been sniped. An air of alarm swept the air, then it was pure chaos.

More people began falling dead and yet no gunshots rang out. Only thuds of soldiers hitting the ground.

"Under the table!" Reece yelled at me.

I crawled under and Reece got beneath another table.

This was a base, how was this even possible?

I was startled when a girl's head and arm fell under my table. Her eyes were glazed and blood poured from a bullet hole in her neck. I was shocked, she was actually dead.

As the noise diminished, I looked at the table across from me and made eye contact with Reece who put his finger up to his lips. He redirected his sight on the steps of the black, combat boots coming up beside my table.

Crap.

I refused to take my eyes off of the boots that circled my table. Suddenly, they stopped.

Oh no…

The man bent down, and I made eye contact with two cold, brown eyes.

I scrambled back out from the table and knocked over a few chairs. They shot at me immediately.

Oh god! Oh god! my mind screamed. I tried the doors and found them locked.

This couldn't be happening!

The bullets continued and I felt them graze me a few times. My shoulder lit up in pain and I dropped to the ground to avoid the second wave. My hand gripped my shoulder. It hadn't gone in, but the bullet had taken a considerable chunk of my flesh with it.

They were on me in an instant, making sure I was pinned securely to the ground. I managed to struggle for what it was worth but lost in a matter of seconds.

My hair was grabbed and pulled back so my neck was exposed. The head guy kneeled beside me and pulled out a syringe full of some sort of yellow liquid.

I jerked my head, freeing myself for a moment, but I was pinned again.

"GET OFF!" I growled.

"Keep him steady," the head guy with the needle said. "It'd be bad if I messed this up."

I thrashed and writhed, but I was already exhausted. Someone, please help me!

The grip on me tightened and I couldn't move.

"That's better." The needle-holding freak soothed as he swabbed the base of my neck. "This won't hurt, I promise."

I wanted to scream. I didn't care if it didn't hurt, I didn't want it.

The prick from the needle told me it had been inserted and I yelped. Unexpectedly, metal met bone with a loud bong, and the hands pinning me were thrown off.

I sat up and saw a frying pan hit the floor along with the needle freak. An angry Reece made eye contact with me.

"RUN!" he yelled.

I stumbled to my feet and began a sharp sprint to him.

"GET OUT OF HERE!"

I turned to the doors that had been locked. How?

Reece read my mind.

"There's a door in the kitchen! Go!"

I nodded then made a break for it. When I opened the kitchen door, I saw the building across the base grounds burst into flames from the bottom up.

What is happening?

Another explosion rumbled and I saw the fire and smoke rise into the air. The infrastructure crumbled to the ground a few seconds later.

Who could've done this? I asked myself, the image of the uniformed men from the past two mornings came to my mind in answer.

I decided to hide in the nearest building. If I flew, I'd abandon Reece. I needed to find a place to wait for an opening so we both could escape. I caught my breath for a few moments when I heard rustling from the other side of the door. I needed to go and now. I turned the corner and ran. I needed a better place to hide.

I ran out through the back exit and into the drizzling rain again.

The door burst open and shouting followed as my pursuers saw me running into a sprint to getaway.

Footsteps caught up to me, and then gunshots. I yelled as the worst pain imaginable exploded in my ankle. I blacked out briefly but woke up to a needle in my neck.

"GaaAAAHHHH!" I screamed.

I reached up and put a hand on my neck.

What was this? The fourteenth time this had happened?

"There, now that wasn't so bad," a voice said.

I tried to focus on who was talking but failed miserably. I knew what they'd put in me, it was a sedative. I felt everything slowing down and unconsciousness creeping closer. It was working immediately.

"I hate you," I spat.

"Sorry fella, but it's for the best."

I fought the darkness off as long as I could, but the drug overcame me.

"Will...Will wake up."

"Is he okay?"

"He should be."

"Hey yo, dude, get your butt up, I know you're awake."

I opened my eyes and saw Reece.

"Reece? Where..."

"Shh, they'll find us."

I looked past him to see John covered in soot and singed clothes. He gave me a small smile.

"We need you to get up, Will," Reece said.

I nodded slowly. It took me a minute to understand what

he meant since my head was still groggy.

He slung my arm over his shoulders, and I winced in pain. We stood up before I had the strength to say anything.

"Ow."

"Sorry pal, you're gonna have to deal with it for now."

"I'm going to get help."

"Be careful, okay, I heard a few gunshots."

The engineer nodded.

"I'm glad you're okay, Ascella, you had me worried there for a sec. Oh, and sorry for the crappy medical job. I only know basic stuff."

I hadn't realized my ankle and shoulder were wrapped until he pointed it out.

"Thanks," I croaked.

He gave a defiant smirk and then it disappeared.

"What happened?" I asked

Reece glanced at me.

"Whoever these people want you. John and I were able to take you back before they put you in their jet to who knows where."

I wanted to laugh at Reece's energy, he was always so animated.

"They're looking for you right now so John and I hid in this building, but we need to move. It could come down at any second.

I smiled. My friend had rescued me.

"Thanks, bro."

"Don't worry about it, but we do need to get outta here."

Reece helped me get through the doorway and down a hallway that rained dust every time the ground shook.

"We need to get to the lower levels so we can avoid getting trapped if this building blo-"

A large boom shook the building and everything went dark except for the red emergency lights.

"Are you okay?" Reece asked.

"Should be."

"We need to hurry, think you can handle some stairs?"

"I'll try."

"This way through the door."

Reece helped me through the door and down the first flight of stairs.

My shoulder ached, but that wasn't as problematic as trying to get my lame ankle to move.

"I think your ankle's shot dude, no pun intended."

"You're the worst."

"Oh please, you lov-"

A rumble cut him off and shook the building. Sounds of creaking metal echoed up the stairs.

"That didn't sound good."

"Nope."

"Let's get to the ground before-"

I looked up and saw it.

"REECE!" I screamed.

The building came down on top of us.

CHAPTER 15

TAKE ME NOT HIM

The seconds it'd happened were the most painful.

He pushed me down the stairs as the rubble came down.

"REECE!" I screamed.

I tumbled down and hit the wall.

"Reece!" I screamed again, tears streaming down my face. "Reece! Please answer me!"

The only answer that came was the settling of the rubble.

My body protested as I stood up. But I staggered to the pile and began to roll off the smaller pieces of cement and drywall. He had to be alive.

A fire began inching down the stairs getting closer. It was below as well but being trapped by flames didn't bother me at the moment.

I kept digging without a second thought. I had to find him. I flinched as my hands became raw, scrapped by the sharper pieces. But I didn't care.

I coughed and gasped for air. The smoke made it difficult to breathe. My fingers brushed something soft.

I dug harder to uncover Reece's leg. Sobbing with pained joy, I pushed the last slab off of him.

For a moment, when I saw him I wasn't sure what to do.

The metal pipes and rods jutting up from his stomach made my mouth go dry.

I checked his pulse, and it was still there. Barely.

Carefully, I looked over the material impaling him.it wasn't anchoring him into place. I picked him up and moved him from the pile of rubble to the area between the flights of stairs. After leaning Reece against the wall, I dropped down beside him. Sweat drops ran down my face as I laid my head against the wall. I felt a sudden weight on my shoulder and saw Reece had fallen against me. I placed my wing around him, protecting him.

"Please don't go," I whispered, lips trembling.

Reece lay unmoving.

I placed my head on his hair and fought the tears in vain.

"You're gonna be okay."

A part of me already knew, but I needed to hear some sort of comfort.

Reece coughed then groaned.

"Reece!"

I sat up and looked at him.

"Thank god! You're alive!"

I couldn't help it. I sobbed and put my hand on his cheek. He grinned painfully.

"It'll be okay, Will," Reece said.

I felt his hand shakily ruffle my hair as I tried to get myself together. I looked at him.

"I won't let you die."

"Don't worry, I won't."

"I'll get help."

"How're you gonna do that?"

Reece's voice was raspy from the smoke.

"I'll crawl."

"Yeah, that'll get ya real far."

I knew Reece was trying to be sarcastic, but I just couldn't laugh. He had a point. Instead, I leaned back against the wall beside him.

We both went silent, and I closed my eyes. I felt Reece

lay his head on my shoulder and I laid my head onto his.

"Remember when we first met?" Reece suddenly asked.

"Yeah."

"I thought you were the scariest kid I'd ever met."

I smiled a little.

"And you spent every lunch with me regardless?"

"Yeah."

Another pause of silence.

Reece began coughing then continued, "By the way, a few days ago, I totally kicked your butt in hand to hand."

"No, you didn't."

"Yeah, I did."

The fire roared and the building rumbled.

"You tripped me and went for my head."

Reece chuckled then coughed and wiped the blood from his mouth, "You stumbled. It gave me an opportunity."

I mustered a small laugh, causing sharp pains in my lungs.

"When we get outta here, I'll go see Peyton and introduce you. I know y'all will hit it off."

"If she's anything like you, I'm sure we would."

"I meant dating."

"Nah, girls scare me."

I felt Reece chuckle briefly

I looked at him smiling away but could only imagine the pain he felt right now.

"Future career?" I asked.

There was a long pause. Reece was dozing.

"Reece?"

His eyes opened and he blinked several times

"I'm gonna be a pilot."

"Why a pilot?"

"So I can see what you see when..." He trailed off leaving me waiting for him to finish. He never did.

"Reece?"

I glanced at my friend who slept peacefully on my shoulder.

"I love you," I whispered. "I'm gonna get you out of here, I don't know how, but I will."

I coughed and found that I couldn't inhale. There wasn't enough oxygen left. I closed my eyes and waited out the pain. My chest felt as if my ribs were being ripped open.

I pulled Reece closer.

At least we were together.

My eyes were closing from exhaustion and dizziness. I was glad the pain was ending and welcomed the darkness.

I awoke to bright light. The voices I heard were an octave too low and my sight wouldn't focus.

I couldn't help but fall back under. When I opened my eyes again, I was in a tent.

The pain all over my body felt like fire. My memories took me back to the building falling and the fire. Had I been burned? I sat up carefully and something slipped out from my hand and dropped to the ground.

I picked it up and held it closer to my face.

It was Reece's dog tag.

Why did I have it? Why wasn't this with him? If I was rescued, then he was too.

I crawled through the tent curtains and hobbled out into the rows of white tents. Nurses and doctors were hustling around with medical supplies or wearing bloodied gloves and scrubs.

"Ascella!"

I made eye contact with a young doctor who ran over

to me. He grabbed my arm and began asking hurried questions. Who was he? Why was he acting this way? Alarms went off in my head.

"Let me go!" I yelled pushing the doctor off. I tripped over my bad leg and fell to the ground. He came closer and I scooted away from him.

"Ascella, please!"

"I've got to find him!"

"Find who?"

"Reece!" I said holding up the dog tag in my hand.

The doctor looked from my hand to my eyes. He sighed as he ran a hand through his greasy hair.

"Your friend's gone."

"No, I was just with him!"

"The man we found you with was dead before we could get to him."

"Liar! He fell asleep!"

"Will, he is dead!"

I fell silent.

"Look I don't know what you've been through, but I'm not lying. Your friend didn't make it. It's a miracle we saved you before you died too."

I stared at him, tears threatening to fall.

"We tried, but we couldn't save him."

"I need to see for myself."

"We... we can't allow you to, besides he was already taken."

The doctor spoke like he was nervous. He was hiding something.

"Where did you take him?"

The doctor looked away and took a breath before saying, "I don't know. I'm not authorized to say."

I couldn't move. What had they done to my best friend? What had I done to my best friend?

"What do you mean you aren't authorized to say?"

"Ascella, I need to look at your wounds."

"No! Don't touch me!" I yelled as he approached.

He called someone on his radio attached to his shoulder.

"I need assistance in Sector 42, Will Ascella is resistant to care."

I glared at him, anger surging through me.

It wasn't even a minute before I saw two male security and a female nurse round the corner heading towards us. The doctor and I held eye contact while they came before us.

"What did you do to Reece?" I growled.

The doctor didn't answer.

The guards reached us, and both of my arms were locked into place as I was led back to the tent I had woken up in. I was laid down and let go since I didn't put up much of a fight.

The nurse and doctors asked the typical questions and checked my vitals before deeming me alright.

"You need to get rest," the doctor said.

"I can rest once I see Reece."

The nurse gave the doctor a questioning look.

"The man we found with Ascella was untreatable. He passed as we were trying to save him."

My eyes narrowed. He changed his story. Earlier, he had said Reece was dead before they'd even got there.

The nurse smiled sadly at me.

"I'm sorry honey," she said. "I know this must be a shock for you."

The small bit of sympathy made the weight come crashing down. I had done my best to hold back my tears, but I failed and sobbed violently.

"No, no, no," I repeated.

"Sweety, it'll be okay. Here, take these for me."

I took the pills without a second thought and the doctor and nurse left. A wave of exhaustion came over me. It must've been from the pills they gave me to put me to sleep. I wanted to stay awake, but eventually I gave in. It was all I could do to prolong the reality that awaited me when I woke up.

I wasn't sure how long I'd been out when I opened my eyes. The feeling in my gut immediately made me lean over and dry heave.

I felt miserable but better. I sat up and looked around. It was dark and quiet, making me think it was probably early morning or late at night. I heard soft footsteps outside. I assumed it was the nurses until I heard a gun load. My brows furrowed as I scooted to the entrance of the tent and peeked outside. I recognized the same black uniforms from my morning runs from the previous two days.

Instead of tools, they held guns. I watched them go in and out of the tents. What were they doing?

I froze when I heard a voice in a tent nearby get cut off by the thud of a silencer.

They were killing people.

Something told me that I was probably next in line if I stuck around. I needed to get out of here. There was a medical box in the corner. I opened it and pulled out a scalpel. Another thud.

Taking the sharp end of the tool, I began slicing a hole through the seam of the tent corner. Once it was big enough, I poked my head out to make sure I wouldn't get shot the moment I stepped outside. I was lucky enough to be facing the back of another tent.

Thud.

Quickly, I slipped out. My ankle protested, but I limped between the tents and the shadows. I froze behind a tent as a pack of men ran by. My eyes lingered on them until they were completely gone then resumed my trek.

"W-who are you?" a voice whispered.

My entire body froze.

Could someone see me?

I looked around and saw no one. I thought I'd maybe imagined it when the voice came again.

I looked at the tent to my right. It was coming from the other side.

"No one," a gruff voice answered.

"Wait, stop! I'll do-"

Thud

My eyes shut tightly as I knew what had happened. Only until there was complete silence again did I move. I took a step, and a bullet came flying at me ripping a hole in the tent's wall. It missed. I turned my head and saw through the hole, an eye glaring at me.

"Don't move," the man said.

Frick that.

I sprinted. My ankle was screaming, but the fear and adrenaline screamed louder. I rounded the corner and turned around to see if I'd lost him.

There were some shots farther away, but some sounded a lot closer. I took cover in a random tent to catch my breath.

As soon as I stepped in I felt a knife at my throat.

"Um, hello?" a female voice asked impatiently.

I looked up and made eye contact with a freckle-faced, blonde girl.

She paused and glanced at my wings, "Will?"

"Uh, yes?"

Did I know her?

"What's going on out there?"

Whoa are we not gonna address how we know each other?

"Uh, there are men outside killing people and I can assume I would've been dead right now had I not taken off."

She nodded, "Those sounds..?"

"Silencers."

"I'll go with you."

"What! No, I don't even know you. Plus, you'll die if you're with me"

"And if I stay here I'd die, too so let's go."

I was speechless. How was I supposed to argue with that?

"Fine. We should go," I grunted.

I got up and checked the environment around us.

"Where are we going?" she asked.

"Anywhere, but here. But preferably out of this death camp."

I crawled out and hobbled beside her until we reached the end of the tents. The city in the distance looked completely ravaged. Smoke filled the sky making the rising sun dull and gray. I was in shock.

"What happened here?" I whispered.

The girl answered me solemnly, "The city was attacked by what was assumed to be terrorists. It was a mass bombing on all of the city's vital personnel."

"What do you mean? And how the heck do you even

know that?"

"Everything essential, like the first responders, the base, airports was all bombed simultaneously. I was leaving the hospital when it blew up. I woke up here, in what I assume is a medical camp."

"You're a citizen?"

"Yeah."

This was going to be worse than I thought.

"So what's the plan?" the blonde asked.

"As of right now, nothing because I can't even find a good hiding place."

She snorted. "Explains why we've been standing here for about a minute now."

I gave her a look. This girl reminded me of Reece.

"Whatever, let's go this way."

A bullet whizzed by us.

How convenient.

The girl and I darted into the street to take over.

Another bullet flew in between us. I could feel it nearly graze my arm. It startled me enough to make me jump to the side. These guys were aiming to kill.

I ducked behind the closest object, an overturned car. I looked around wondering where the girl had gone, then I saw her. She was ducking behind a fallen wall on the other side of the street. I needed to get back with her, she had nothing to defend herself. I got up readying myself for a sprint over to her. A rain of bullets against the car stopped me. I crouched back down pressing my back against the car.

I could feel the bullets sinking into the metal and heard the glass shattering.

Please don't explode! Please don't explode!

The shooting stopped and a man appeared around the

edge. I pulled out my scalpel. I swung up at his eyes and disarmed him. I quickly knocked him over the head and added a gun to my inventory. Inching my head around the car, I glimpsed the enemy.

I stepped out slowly putting my hands up in surrender.

The man was holding the girl hostage. He grinned upon my reaction.

"Put the gun down, Ascella."

I looked at the girl then back to him.

"If I do, will you let her go?" I asked

"I promise not to hurt her," the man said.

Not ideal, but I wasn't in the position to argue.

"Alright, I'll hold you to that," I said, slowly putting the gun on the ground. The girl suddenly yelled, "No! Will! Run!"

As soon as I'd released the gun, they pounced. My hands were tied and my mouth gagged.

I was shoved against the side of the car where the girl sat with her hands bound.

"Why?" she whispered. "Why didn't you run?"

I looked at her. Did she think I was going to let her die?

Suddenly, a hand grabbed my shirt and yanked me up. I came face to face with a face that made the Ugly Duckling look pretty.

"You sure they want him? The kid's half-dead, if ya ask me."

He let go and I fell back against the car.

"Yeah, HQ made a big deal 'bout him, remember? Go get the truck."

I could only imagine who their "HQ" was.

After the dude left, it was only a couple of minutes before I heard the rumbling of an engine.

I glanced at the truck that rolled up to me. A few men jumped out and came over to me. I glared at them coldly as they grabbed my arms. The girl began to protest but was thrown back against the truck. I was lifted and walked to the open doors. Glancing back, the girl looked terrified.

It angered me. All of it, Reece was dead, this girl was going to be subjected to whatever tortures these men wanted and it was because of me.

A rush of energy spread throughout my body. My anger fueled it until it was as strong as the other times.

I jerked my body away from their grip and planted my feet. I refused to go any further. The men grunted as they fought with me.

"Hey, Conner! help us out, would ya!"

I swung my wing and took out the guy on my left. He flew back with a yell. Another man replaced him and sent me to my knees after an impact on my head. I took a knife from his waistband and freed myself. Then I gripped his arm and threw a left hook at his face. He blocked me and knocked the blade from my grip. An attack came from behind. I spun, ramming my elbow into my attacker's neck. He fell and two more men came.

There were too many for me to keep up. It was pathetic. This girl was depending on me.

Suddenly, my legs were kicked out from under me. My head slammed into the ground, and I was barely conscious as I felt the men tying my wings and feet.

Suddenly, there was a scream and gunshots. One of the men dropped to the pavement beside me. His eyes were glazed, and blood trickled out of his mouth.

"He's over there! Grab the girl!" was the last thing I heard before I passed out.

CHAPTER 16

I MESSED UP

"Don't touch me," I hissed.

"We're not trying to hurt you."

I narrowed my eyes completely skeptical of the man that spoke. I'd woken up surrounded by FBI-looking agents. The girl was nowhere to be found and I was suffering from random spikes of adrenaline and the crashes that came afterward. I glared at the men failing to hide their nervous glances.

It'd be simple to free myself from the ropes around my wrists, but the real problem was being in the truck. Suddenly, the vehicle slowed to a stop and built up speed again. My hands were untied, and I finally worked up the nerve to ask about the blonde girl.

"Where is she?"

"Different truck," the man on my left grunted.

Why were they separating me from her?

I leaned back against the wall and sighed.

"We'll get ya fixed up when we stop."

I nodded in response.

I wasn't worried all that much about my injuries, but rather where this truck was going to take me to get me "fixed up."

I stared at the dimly lit floor. It was an attempt to avoid the glances and stares I continued to receive. It was silent which didn't do much of anything but allow me to contemplate.

I leaned forward resting my head on my hands.

"What do you want from me?"

"What?"

"What do you want from me?" I asked again.

"We don't want anything from you Will, we're trying to protect you."

I scoffed, "Why would-"

The truck halted to a stop. Everyone fell back. Footsteps came crunching on gravel moments before the doors swung open.

"We've arrived, but get him out of here!"

"What's going on?"

"The terrorists they're-"

The poor guy didn't get to even finish his answer before a bullet went through his head.

The male next to me cursed, "They must've followed us here."

The soldiers poured out and I was quickly helped off.

"Get Ascella out of here!" one shouted.

"Why are they this close to our base?" another said.

"These terrorists don't stop!"

The outbursts of the soldiers were all I heard as I limped towards the towering building ahead.

The male next to me began muttering about how slow of a pace we were going.

I was going to suggest letting me walk on my own and the rest of them get to safety, when suddenly he spoke, "Sorry Will," then he picked me up.

"Put me down!" I yelled.

I pulled my wings in to avoid getting stepped on.

As we made a break for the doors, I tensed as we tumbled in. Immediately, nurses surrounded us, and I was pulled away from the soldier who leaned up against the wall panting.

He spoke to the nurses making several glances and gestures at me. He gave me one last look then smirked.

"See ya around kid," he said.

After that, the guy stood up, pulled out his gun then ran through the doors into the chaos outside.

A nurse came up to me. "Give us a moment and we'll have a room prepped for you."

I nodded absently and watched the doors the man had just run through.

"What is this place?" I asked, looking around.

"This is our medical unit, we're The Council," the nurse answered. "We were a nonprofit organization, but since the attacks, we've had to fill the gaps left in the emergency services."

"I see."

I glanced at the symbol that was engraved into the wall behind the receptionist's desk and was shocked. I recognized the stacked triangles making one large triangle. It was the same thing I'd seen on the coin General Gray had been messing with when he'd had that weird talk with me. Something was off.

The two nurses helped me into the elevator and get into an open room on the second floor.

"What are ya'll?" I asked.

One of the nurses glanced at me puzzled.

"What do you mean?" she asked.

"Are you… were you part of the government?"

The nurse chuckled.

"Oh no, we're operated on by a private charity. But we did recently step into a government-like position. Many officials have come to us for aid since the legislative branch was wiped out."

This was all odd, Gray didn't seem to be the charity type of guy in my opinion. And how did a third of the government fall in just one day?

The nurses helped me lie down. The bed was like any other hospital bed, stiff.

"I'll make sure a doctor comes and looks at your foot and gives you a full analysis," one of them said.

They left, so after a few minutes I got up and checked out the small room.

Suddenly, my door burst open, and I nearly jumped out of my skin.

"Will!"

I looked at the brown-haired nerd gaping at me.

"John?" I breathed.

A smile ghosted my lips. I couldn't be more thankful to see a familiar face.

"You don't know how happy I am to see you!" he exclaimed, running over and embracing me. "I was afraid you and Reece wouldn't make it out."

I froze.

"The nurses said something about a winged boy and I knew it was you! But hey, do you know where they put Reece, I've got some good news for him."

My face was covered by his hug, so he didn't see the tears threatening to fall.

"I'm sorry," I said.

He pulled away and looked at me.

I averted my gaze quickly. How could I look at him?

"Will? Where's Reece?"

Something told me he knew, but I still couldn't look at him yet. When I glanced up, John was staring blankly at the ground.

"I'm so sorry," I whispered. "I tried to ask where they'd taken him but..."

I couldn't speak about it anymore, so I reached into my pocket and pulled out the dog tag.

"No..." he said, "no, no, no."

John plopped down onto the hospital bed burying his head in his hands.

"What am I gonna tell Payton?" he groaned.

Payton.

I'd totally forgotten.

How could I have forgotten Reece's sister?

"I'm sorry," I whispered quietly. "I tried but there was nothing I could do to-"

"What happened?" John said apathetically.

I hung my head as I recounted the dreadful memory.

"Reece was helping me get to the bottom floor so we wouldn't get trapped in the building. But there was a bomb, and it all came down. We were on the stairwell...I thought he'd just fallen asleep, I swear, but the doctors said-"

"Screw what the doctors said, Will what do you think happened?"

I was confused. What did he mean?

"Sorry?" I asked.

John averted his eyes, "Will, I'm gonna tell you something that I haven't told anyone. But you know how I'm one of the younger heads in I.T? I've seen some very weird things going on about Reece."

"What do you mean weird?"

"I'm just gonna say it, I think Reece was murdered during these attacks or whatever."

My mind felt as if it had completely stopped.

"I saw messages and these guys that were working on

the base gave me some real mixed messages. But I honestly don't know."

Silence hung heavily in the air. Things came to my mind, almost as if I was metaphorically trying to put together a puzzle. General Gray was at the center of it. The odd questions he asked, the weird responses he gave. The man possibly had a motive, but I couldn't explain it. Something wasn't connecting.

"Payton's here. Wanna go see her?" John asked.

"She's gonna ask."

"She's gotta know."

I nodded.

"Come on, then."

John stood up and led me out the door. As I followed him into the elevator, my palms grew sweaty. What was I gonna say to her?

We got off on the fourth floor and walked down the hall. There was a glass window in the wall and John looked through it. He stopped abruptly and turned.

"The blonde one," he said.

I followed his gaze.

I stopped short as I looked at her. It was the same girl I'd met in the medical camp. There had to have been a mistake.

The girl was helping a few nurses put together food and medical packets.

"That can't be her."

"What do you mean?" John asked.

"I've already met her."

"What? How?"

"We were in the same medical camp, I bumped into her on the run, and she came with me."

"Did she know who you were?"

"I mean she knew my name."

"Did she ask about Reece?"

"No."

I looked back at Payton's smiling face. The news I brought with me would only cause that smile to go away.

I turned away. John followed me back to the elevator.

"Where are you going?"

"I can't face her."

"Will, you don't have to-"

"No, John, really. I should've died that day, not Reece."

My friend went silent. It felt as if he was agreeing with me.

Luckily, the elevator doors slid shut and I was alone. I got out and walked back to my room and laid down again.

"Why am I alive but you're not?" I asked while looking up at my ceiling. I could envision my best friend looking down, shaking his head, and shrugging, "Why did you save me? Why didn't you get yourself out of the way?"

I probably sounded crazy talking out loud, but I didn't care.

The shy grin on that freckled face was easy to imagine.

"If it was switched around, we would have both been with our families."

I rolled over and looked at the wall until my eyes closed. When I came to, I got up and opened the window to let in the air. The sun poured through casting a golden hue over my room.

An idea popped into my head, and I judged how hard it would be to take off from the window. Not bad, but not ideal. I looked down at my ankle. It wasn't hurting that bad and the doctor was taking his sweet time.

Should I at least tell John? Nah, I should be back before anyone notices.

I gave myself the all-clear and leapt from the window, working to get myself up into the air. The air was much cooler, preventing me from working up a sweat.

The rush of air calmed me down allowing me to think.

How am I going to tell her? Can I be upfront with it? I practiced in my head what I wanted to say.

The dense trees changed to a field, and I admired its beauty. Some birds flew past me, and I could almost feel their questioning looks. I went back to my thoughts when something flew by my foot. Immediately, I looked down at the dark figure crouched on the ground.

ARE YOU KIDDING ME?! IT HASN'T EVEN BEEN TEN MINUTES!

Soaring down, I took cover in a tree hoping the person would lose interest.

The footsteps crunched on the brush below and slowed as they got closer.

Could he see me? Surely not, this is one thick tree.

The guy came into view, and I quickly sized him up. I could take him. He turned his back to me and pulled out a pistol. I took my chance and dropped from the tree and threw a punch and a knee to his face. He screamed and fell attempting to recover.

I picked up the pistol he'd dropped and aimed it at him.

"Who are you and why are you after me?"

He didn't answer but instead whipped his head to my right.

Were there more of them?

I was relieved that it was a false alarm, but I'd given him an opening. The taser hit me before I could react.

I grunted and fell to the ground groping for the gun.

"Black in four! Back up now!" I heard the man shout into his radio.

Great, now his buddies were actually gonna be here.

The gun was kicked away from my hand and the man stood over me triumphantly. I landed the nut shot so perfectly, I wanted to writhe for him. The dude fell and let out a gut-wrenching scream.

You had that coming, sir.

I got up and made a break for it. I couldn't beat them outnumbered. I needed to get back.

If I take off from the field I could get back to the hospital in less-

The hair on the back of my neck. Multiple gunshots fired behind me as I ducked. Getting back up again, I jumped a bush and rolled down a small hill. My ankle screamed in discomfort.

I glanced back and saw them getting closer.

To my right, an engine roared and a black dirt bike broke through the trees cutting me off.

I staggered to a stop and kept my eyes on my pursuers. They slowed and circled around me.

I narrowed my eyes looking for an opening, but they seemed to be good at this. I couldn't take off either, the trees were too thick and they'd probably shoot me before I could get off the ground.

The person cut the engine on the bike and hopped off. They came over to me and pulled a pistol out and pressed the barrel against my forehead and pushed me backward until my spine hit a tree.

Were they gonna kill me?

The person lifted their helmet visor and I saw a woman

underneath.

"You've got some real explaining to do, Ascella," my old drill sergeant yelled.

It was at that moment I knew I'd messed up.

CHAPTER 17

GRANDMA'S CONDEMNING COOKIES

"They're a charity, not some underground ruler," I said.

"Oh, is that what they told you?" my drill sergeant asked, still holding the gun to my head.

I gave her a look as two guys came forward. A box was in their hands. The man on my right pulled out a small package and unwrapped a syringe. It was filled with liquid then the guy carefully stuck the needle in my neck. By now, I didn't even flinch.

"What was that?"

"A sedative. You'll be out shortly."

"Wow," I said sarcastically.

I could already feel my body numbing. I slid down the trunk of the tree into a squat. My eyes focused on my drill sergeant as a wave of betrayal hit me. It reminded me to never trust anyone, otherwise, situations like this would only repeat.

That was the last thought I had before my consciousness was gone.

I awoke with a blindfold and a gag in my mouth. I resisted the urge to panic and focused. Testing the restraints, I found that they'd done a crappy job. If they were going to kidnap someone they'd better improve some things. My hands groped around to feel my surroundings and I touched a corner. A metal shelf maybe? Whatever it was, it was useful to help get my blindfold off.

Once I'd gotten it moved up enough for me to see, I was shocked.

The utility closet would not have been my first choice

to put someone, but kudos to them for trying, I thought, glancing around at the various mops and brooms. Overall, I would've given them a solid four if I was rating my kidnapping experience.

Suddenly, the door swung open, and two men came in. We made eye contact and they chuckled.

"Sorry kid, but you wouldn't have gotten far."

I made a low grunt in response.

The uglier one came and hoisted me up, while the other fixed my blindfold.

Wonderful, back to darkness.

Relying only on hearing, I tried to figure out where I was. After I heard some doors open and close, my footsteps began to echo. The eerie feeling came over me that I had entered a large room and many, many eyes were looking at me.

A pair of hands pushed down on my shoulders forcing me to sit. Next, my blindfold and gag were taken off.

When I looked around, a hundred people were staring at me. The colosseum-like room was intimidating enough, but the old woman standing across from me sent chills down my spine.

The woman had bobbed hair and a blue blazer. Her most notable feature was her smile that defined fake. That must've taken a lot of Botox.

"Will Ascella," Ms. Grandma purred. "I'm glad to see you've survived, though not surprising. I have a few questions for you."

I swallowed, "Uh, okay."

The woman walked closer to me with a glint in her eyes. "Do you know General Arthur Gray?"

I paused, "Obviously."

The woman, who I guessed was old enough to be baking cookies for grandchildren, bent down closer to my face. Her perfume was disgusting.

"How well did you know him? Did he ever approach you individually?"

"I didn't know him outside of a general soldier relationship."

Something in me warned me that I ought to be guarded. Ms. Grandma paced in front of me.

"Did you ever talk to him alone?"

"No," I lied.

She glanced at a man who was writing something down while nodding.

"Mr. Ascella, did you know beforehand about the attack? Did you know what that attack was going to do to our military, our loved ones, our country?"

I looked at her. Did she think this was my fault?

"No."

"You sound confident."

Well here's a shocker, maybe I am confident, Grandma.

The woman got closer to me, giving me another whiff of her suffocating perfume.

"Interesting," the woman hissed. "You are David Ascella's son, are you not?"

I was shocked at the mention of my dad. Why did that matter to them? Did they know my dad?

"Well?"

"Yes," I answered quietly.

The woman turned to the people watching the interrogation. There were papers being passed around the audience.

"If you look at the second page," Ms. Grandma said,

addressing the crowd, "you'll see a criminal record of David Ascella, Will Ascella's father, who was one of the founders of The Council that has attacked this country."

Whoa, hold up, what?

There was silence before the first person stood up.

"This is outrageous!" the man shouted. "If the father made that filthy organization and the son's in it, he's just as guilty!"

"I agree with Mr. White!"

"I concur!"

"Yes! Keep the boy and The Council separate!"

I looked around in horror as the people grew angrier and angrier looking at whatever was on that paper.

The old woman held up her hands and the room gradually grew silent.

"I agree with you all, we cannot stand by and allow The Council to take over this country or any others in the same manner. I suggest we take away their greatest asset. If we cripple them now, we can disband them."

The room erupted into applause and shouting. I had no idea what was happening, but a bad feeling began to fester in my gut.

"Men, take him outside, we need to discuss what our next step will be."

I didn't want to leave. Not when they were more than likely about to discuss what they were doing with me. But I was removed and found myself outside standing between the ugly guy from earlier and his sidekick.

A good thirty minutes passed before the double doors clicked and men and women started streaming out. Some cast glances at me, while others refused to look at me at all.

The last out of the door was Ms. Grandma. She pulled

the men aside one by one talking to them in low tones. It made me suspicious and a little anxious.

They glanced at me, then nodded at her before gripping my arms and dragging me down the hall.

"Where are we going?"

"Outside."

"Why?"

"Shut up."

I was ushered down a stairwell and out of the building. We went around, back where a green river was slowly drifting.

"Are you going to kill me?" I asked.

When neither of them looked at me, I knew that was exactly what they planned to do. I couldn't believe it. That grandma, who should've been baking cookies for grandchildren, had baked and served her own recipe called Condemnation to Death.

My body reacted to the panic that overwhelmed me. I plowed my feet into the ground refusing to go further.

My adrenaline kicked in as the goosebumps spread on my arms and neck.

I threw my wing into Ugly catching him by surprise.

"What the-" he yelled.

I turned and kicked Sidekick. He threw a fist and I ducked to avoid it.

"Shoot him!" Sidekick yelled.

Ugly pulled out his pistol and I jumped behind Sidekick just as the gun went off. Maybe I should've nicknamed Ugly, Stupid.

Sidekick yelled in pain and clutched his shoulder.

"You shot me!" Sidekick cried.

"Then get out of the way!" Ugly yelled at him.

Wow, great teamwork guys.

Ugly grabbed my wrist and I used a high kick to occupy his other hand giving me a freebie. I swung my wing over and connected my joint to his temple. The jar to my joint left me with a sting afterward.

The man stumbled back and held his head.

Suddenly, a fist came outta nowhere and connected with my jaw. I clutched my face instantly.

I looked up at Sidekick standing above me with a smug look on his face.

"What?" I spat.

"A mouse tryna fight two cats ain't gonna win."

I rolled my eyes.

First, he needed to work on his evil vibes. Secondly, he left himself wide open. Hitting his goods with a kick, he grabbed his crotch and screamed.

Yeah, that's right-

I ducked the moment the gun went off, luckily it missed.

Ugly was pointing his barrel at me and clutching his temple.

"Die, brat."

He pulled the trigger several more times causing me to kick in my skills from elementary dodgeball. The difference? This was a more serious game called dodge-bullet.

He was reloading when I got ready to send him down too, suddenly a hand grabbed my ankle.

I looked down at Sidekick, he was still on the ground curled into a ball.

Then something cold pressed against my head.

Crap.

Slowly, I turned to Ugly pushing the pistol against my forehead.

I was caught.

"This time. I'm not going to miss."

I looked at him, then closed my eyes accepting it. The gunshot filled my ears.

CHAPTER 18

I HAVE BIG SLEEVES

I opened my eyes. Ugly had been reaching for me. Blood trickled down the corner of his mouth and his forehead. A bullet hole was right between his eyes. He fell back dead as Sidekick looked at me in horror.

I looked back where the bullet came from and saw a unit of men stalking towards us. Suddenly, Sidekick pulled my leg out from underneath me and I fell. He pinned me and took me into a choke hold while pressing the gun against my temple.

We faced the men approaching us and they stopped.

"Come any closer and I'll shoot!" He yelled.

I clawed at his grip. The men were obviously here to get me out of this mess by their reactions.

"Move and I'll shoot him here!"

He dragged me back inside and spoke into his radio as he marched me down the hall.

"Keep moving," he growled.

This was my chance, I had someone here to get me out I just had to get away. Spinning around, I threw a jab at the man who blocked it. The gun went off making a hole in the ceiling. Sidekick snarled and hit my throat. Oxygen escaped from my lungs and for a moment I stumbled back unable to breathe. Sidekick came after me and I sidestepped, barely avoiding him.

My eyes scanned the room until they landed on a pile of piping. It wasn't ideal but it'd have to do. Suddenly, the building shook, sending Sidekick and I to the ground.

That couldn't be good.

Grabbing the pipe, I ripped it out with one good pull. It came loose and the momentum threw me back into Sidekick. Luckily, the back of the pipe hit him in the face. It had been an accident, but it was the best accident so far. As Sidekick stood back up, I got into a fighting stance. The building shook again.

What was going on out there?

Suddenly, Sidekick tackled me. We both hit the ground and I grunted as I swung the pipe into his back. He yelled and grabbed my wrist. I bucked my hips and switched our positions, but he used his weight to pin me back down. Sidekick pulled out a knife with his other hand and brought it down at my face. I barely dodged it as it nicked my ear. It stung with unbelievable fire. As painful as it was, I focused on keeping the knife at bay. We had each other locked.

"You're making this hard," Sidekick grunted.

"You think I'd make it easy?" I retorted.

Quickly, I twisted my torso and used my wings to roll out from him. He lunged at me and I quickly caught his wrist and turned the blade inwards. He yelled as the knife pierced his skin. Sidekick rolled over with a groan and shakily stood up. I raised the pipe and swung it at his head. After a sharp clank, Sidekick fell to the ground with a thud.

I leaned against the wall and caught my breath.

Was he dead?

I gripped the pole and walked cautiously over to him. The man was still breathing. Even though I'd gone through some desensitizing at the base, I didn't want to kill someone unless I had to.

The pistol that Sidekick had dropped earlier was beside my foot. Picking it up, I shoved it into my waistband. I'll keep the pipe for now, it was actually useful. Turning, I made my way down an empty hallway.

Where was everyone?

The sound of fighting caught my attention. It came from the other side of a corner. I stalked up to it, keeping quiet. I wanted to take a look.

Suddenly, a man collided into me.

"You!!" he yelled.

"You!" I yelled back as I swung the pipe.

The crack of his head was all I needed to hear before jumping over him and taking care of his friend. She pulled out her gun and pointed it at me.

I ducked as she pulled the trigger and swiped her legs. The pipe hit the base of her neck and she went limp. I looted the pistols they had and ran.

As I sprinted down the hall, I looked for an exit but there wasn't one. Suddenly, a pair of doors caught my attention and I had to back pedal.

The double doors were wide open, letting me see the inside of the room I'd been condemned in. There were figures inside fighting each other.

I saw a gray uniform take down the black one. He cried out and I froze. It was John.

My eyes began to water as I took off. I pulled out the pistol and loaded it. As far as I was concerned, I wasn't letting another friend of mine die.

The engineer saw me moments before I slammed into the man.

My elbow slammed into the dude's face. I put a bullet in his head before spinning around and taking on another opponent.

"Run!" I shouted at my friend.

"No! We're getting you out!"

"John!"

But it was too late, John stumbled back from the jab he'd received. I rushed at the man with adrenaline. I was locked into a fist fight within moments.

"Your gun!" I yelled at the engineer.

"I might hit you!"

I scrambled to the man into a deadlock. But he knew what I was doing. A shot went off and I tasted bitter salt as his blood sprinkled my face.

Well, that's disgusting.

I turned and saw John exhale. Spitting out as much foreign blood as possible, I glanced around the room for any more threats.

"Dude, I'm so glad I didn't get you," John said.

"I wouldn't have complained," I replied.

"Shut up, we need to get you out of here."

"What about everyone else?"

"They'll be fine, our main goal was to take you back from A.E.R.O."

"Arrow? Like a bow and arrow?"

I saw the smirk John tried to hide. He knew I was doing it on purpose.

"Follow me and turn off your red eye thingy, you look like you're about to kill someone."

"I might be about to kill someone."

John paused.

"Granted."

I chuckled and followed him through the doorway and down a hall. We picked up our pace and ran out a pair of double doors. We'd made it outside.

"You're right!" John yelled.

I drew the pistol and got rid of the attacker quickly.

"Where to?" I asked.

"There's a chopper past the river."

I rounded the corner and pulled my friend back just in time for the spray of bullets to miss us.

"Well, shoot," John muttered.

I looked at the river and the building then got an idea.

"Follow me," I said, turning and running back inside.

It'd be a risk, but it would get us past the river. Plus, it'd be the quickest way.

"Wait, where are we going?!"

"Just run! And take this," I said, tossing him the other pistol.

I rounded the corner back into the trial room and shot the two coming towards us.

John shot a third.

"John! What are you doing?! What is he still doing here?" a Council soldier yelled.

"There's too many outside!" I answered.

John followed me down a hall until I stopped.

"Where are the stairs?" I asked.

"Why do you need the stairs?" he panted.

"I can fly us over them."

"WHAT!"

"Trust me. I can handle it."

John shrugged, "Alright, let me pull up a map of the building."

He pulled out a device and pulled an antenna out of a compartment.

"What is that?"

"It's a scanner I built." He paused. "This way."

I followed him as he led me through an entryway into a

foyer.

"Through that door."

We opened it and headed up the stairs. As we climbed the levels, our breathing got harder.

"Will!"

I turned and saw John bent over catching his breath.

"You hear that?"

I held my breath and strained my ears over the pounding of my pulse.

There were sounds of voices.

I readied my gun and stalked towards the door with a yellow eight painted on it.

"Be careful," John said behind me.

I took an inhale and swung the door open into chaos. I fired my pistol immediately and took out a few guys before slamming the door again.

"The pipe!" I yelled.

John tossed it to me, and I thrust the piece of metal through the handle and lodged it between the railing.

"That's not gonna hold them for long," John muttered.

"I know, but it'll buy us some time."

I began heading up the next flight of stairs.

"Come on!"

We hadn't made up to the next floor when we heard the door fly open.

Footsteps closed in on us as John and I skipped steps to keep ahead.

"He's got a machete!" John yelled at me.

I looked back.

"That's a freaking sword!" I yelled, as I stopped.

"What are you doing?!" John yelled at me.

"Go! I'll hold them back!"

"No!"

I didn't have time to argue as I aimed and fired. Machete Man side stepped and let one of his men take it.

He glared at me before charging.

"Look out!" John yelled.

The blade grazed my cheek as I tried to dodge. Machete Man smirked, clearly pleased with himself. He took another swipe and I dodged it and retaliated with a jab into his stomach. He stumbled down a few stairs barely keeping his balance. Machete Man cursed and barreled up the stairs at me again.

I needed to get rid of this guy, I noted as I cupped my bleeding cheekbone.

"You okay?" John asked from the top of the stairs.

I turned and looked at him, "Do I look okay?"

We passed another floor when I realized we were only going to be trapped if they caught us before getting to the top.

"Go on up, if I'm not there in five, then get out of here," I said.

"Will, no!"

"I said go!"

I made sure John was a flight ahead before turning back to those chasing us. I propelled down the stairs and straight into the Machete Man and his men. The force caused us all to go tumbling down the stairs. I quickly peeled myself off and sprinted through the door to the twelfth floor.

They were problematic. I had to get rid of them.

Lights flickered giving the floor a strobe light effect.

Footsteps came from behind me, and I saw Machete Man. He was followed by only a couple of his men.

I went through some doors and found myself in a conference room.

Crud, I was trapped.

I slid under the table and prayed it was dark enough to give me cover for a few moments until I figured my next move.

Feet came walking in and lapped the table.

The feet turned and began to walk back towards the door. The door then closed.

The feet came straight up to the table and crouched. I panicked as Machete Man crouched down and looked at me.

"Hey, Ascella, come on out, okay?" he cooed.

Surprisingly, I crawled out. What was I supposed to do?

"You really are a pain."

I would've made a comeback, but his hands were already around my throat and my back had been pressed to the floor. He pulled out his big knife and held it up to my face.

"Sorry, bub."

I pulled the trigger.

The man jolted as the bullet went through his stomach and looked at me.

"Smart kid," he grunted, then he fell to the floor beside me. I got up and examined the hole in my clothing. I took the gun from my pocket and reloaded it.

I pried the blade from the guy's hand and rubbed my neck imagining the bruises.

Now, to the roof. I stepped over Machete Man and came to the door that he'd closed. Once outside, I saw that all the henchmen were gone, but where to? I walked down the hallway and turned left at the fork.

"Fate must like me," I mumbled.

The window ahead of me was big enough and the glass looked like crap so it had to be old. I picked up my pace and unfurled my wings. I pulled the trigger and jumped capsuling myself in my wings.

Unfurling my wings, I caught myself and made my way up to the roof where I saw John standing there watching me circle around.

"Hold out your hands!" I yelled.

The engineer paused, then ran to the edge doing as I asked.

"Alright, here we go," I muttered.

I dove forward and outstretched my hands. Pain flared in my right wing as I lost control. Luckily, I hit the concrete and rolled to the edge.

"Will!" John yelled.

I groaned and looked at my wing. The bullet wound looked bad. Blood was beginning to gush from it making it hard to tell if it was a graze or if there was a piece of lead stuck in me.

John ran over to me, horror etched onto his face as he saw the wound.

"Will! Are you alright?"

I slid my throbbing joint over to him as he knelt down beside me.

John exhaled, "I think it's a graze, but it's deep."

My relief was short lived as I realized we were stuck up here with no escape route.

"Ascella, what a pleasure to see you again," a familiar voice greeted me.

I looked up and saw Ms. Grandma step out from the shadows. She wiped her pistol down with a handkerchief. I connected the dots and hated her even more if that was possible.

"I can't say the same," I sneered.

"I see you've brought your little Council friend. Who are you sweetie?"

John put himself between us and stood up to her eye level.

"You're not touching him."

Her eyes bounced from her gun to John then me.

She smiled, "Wouldn't dream of it."

"Miss Roslytch!"

My eyes focused on a young man followed by others that filed out from the staircase.

"Miss Roslytch! Are you alright?!" he asked, coming over to the old woman as if she was possibly hurt.

Bro, I'm the one on the ground.

He glanced at the situation and one swift motion of his hand had us cornered. On every side we were at gunpoint.

Wonderful.

I glared at the grandma as I managed to get back on my feet with John's help. Roslytch turned to the young officer coddling her.

"Would you mind getting rid of them, darling?"

The young man smirked, "Yes, ma'am."

"Oh, thank you, Charles," Grandma Roslytch said as she turned and placed a peck on his cheek.

It took every fiber of my being not to throw up then and there. She turned and walked back through the staircase's doorway. The click of her heels echoed as she descended.

Once she'd passed through, the young officer made a motion with his hand.

"Ready, men!"

I glanced behind me at the drop off that awaited John

and I. It wasn't too bad, but it wasn't great. It would it be suicide if I jumped, but even that sounded better than getting loaded up by bullets.

My eyes glanced at the windows. Some were broken which gave me an idea.

"Aim!"

Sorry, Grandma, but I had one last trick up my sleeve.

"John, do you trust me?" I asked, scooting closer to the edge.

The engineer looked at me and nodded. I looked back to the young man who was still directing the men. Finally, he gave the order.

"Fire!"